"No feats of heroism
are needed to achieve
the greatest and most important changes
in the existence of humanity;
neither the armament of millions of soldiers...
nor revolutions, nor barricades,
but a change in public opinion.

And to accomplish this...
it is only needful that each individual
should say what he really feels or thinks,
or at least that he should
not say
what he does not think."

Leo Tolstoy

Jessie's Foreword

One of my early childhood memories was of my mother taking me and my sisters to sing at a prolife rally. The lady in charge handed me a tiny pin. She explained that it was a replica of a baby's feet at 15 weeks gestation. I remember cherishing that pin, thinking how sweet the little feet looked.

My understanding wasn't deep enough to grasp the significance of everything that was said that day... and yet, looking back as a mother of seven little ones, it is an event that I am so humbled to have been a part of at such a young age. My perspective has widened beyond the "pretty little pin" to what they represent. That life is precious... no matter how small, no matter how frail, no matter...And the term "pro-life" now encompasses for me so much more than simply the issue of abortion.

Pro-life is a worldview that affects each one of us who have been blessed with "life". Each has value and every one is a gift.

No exceptions.

Jessica Jespersen

February 2011

Stephanie's Foreword

Who doesn't love a baby? We start life as small and cuddly and appealing as we'll ever be, and it's so easy for us to love these tiny little ones. At the same time, for each little baby those early days are teaching them about love – how enmeshed it is with dependency, how overwhelming need can feel, and how sweetly satisfying it is to have those needs met.

Watching this book be written has been a revelation. While the subject matter begins with those easiest to love, it branches into directions that we all take as we grow in love. Where we begin to see the value in every created person, instead of just the one we love best.

Most satisfying for me is the underlying sense of need, and the satisfaction of having, again, a relationship with that One person who is comfort and satisfaction. And again, from that safe, connected place, to be able to embrace others.

Paige is my baby sister, and this book has grown out of her experiences and thoughts as we've grown from three sisters to become three mothers of twenty one children between us. God has blessed us in giving us sisters who love each other and who are willing to share life honestly. My prayer is that this book can be a place for you to join the conversation about God's plan for human life, and His delight in His creation.

Stephanie Fehler

February, 2011

...

for the great great

grandchildren

of

Cairo, Sloan,

Peyton, Charter, Mollen,

Gage and Ephraim

...

40

WEEKS

by

paige beselt

PART I

Thursday, September 6th, 2007

I'm not even pregnant.

I got home from work tonight and I found this package –
from Jack – sitting on the table.   He wasn't home. I knew he
was working night shift tonight.   We just miss each other on
nights like this, but he left the lights on.   Every single light in
the house was burning.   He has a hard time telling me he loves
me in words, but he knows I have begun to hate the dark and
that I would laugh when I saw the whole house lit up like that.
He even left the tiny light in our closet on.   So, I'll take that *'I
love you'* and I'll tuck it in my pocket along with the thousand
others like it.

He left the stew bubbling in the crock pot and the
wrapped package on the table.   When I opened it, I found this
pregnancy journal... and a box of my favourite black pens, the
ones with the fine felt tips.

I feel bereft of words.   I'm incapable of expressing where
I have been – and where I now find myself.   I feel odd writing in
a journal with a picture of a rounded belly on the cover – and
the words, "40 weeks" inscribed beneath.   I have always been
the wordy one – finishing Jack's sentences if he pauses too
long, writing him long love letters and filling his ears with
chatter the moment he walks in the door.   He told me he
'misses my noise'.   My silence is as new and unfamiliar to me
as it is to him – and I wonder if the noisy me has departed for
good.   Part of me feels like forcing laughter at his constant
teasing and letting myself fall back into our normal patter.
And yet, I feel like it would be the most offensive lie to try to act
like I'm the woman I was, when I know I'm just not her
anymore.

So, I'll write.   I'll write for the husband I can't speak to.

I have been a mess lately and I know it.   I can't seem to
get my feet back under me.   Jack knows I'm lost, but he seems

a little lost too and in this darkness, it has seemed impossible to find each other. Silence winds around our evenings till it's so thick, we turn on the television to escape its stifling oppression.

I lost our baby.

Even writing that, I feel the shame flood my body and my leaden hand finds it difficult to even pen the words. I know that Jack gave me this journal as a sign of hope. He keeps saying that we'll try again – that we'll have a baby... and while there's a part of me that believes him, there's another part that just doesn't want to let go of my first baby. The baby I feel like I failed. The baby I lost.

It has been two months. Two months and I still don't know how I'm supposed to act. Sometimes it amazes me that I can be walking around, going to work, coming home, cleaning house... continuing on like nothing happened – when my womb became a tiny coffin. Seems my body doesn't quite know how it's supposed to act either. I have been avoiding going back to the doctor, but I'm starting to wonder if there's something not quite right.

Kind of adds a great big sigh on a sea of sadness.

So, there it is. The first pages of my pregnancy journal filled in. A journal that should be filled with expectancy has begun in sorrow.

Friday, September 7th, 2007

I'm proud of you. – Jack

Sunday, September 9th, 2007

I want to name our baby. I didn't know at the time that it would matter to me, but it does. Nobody asks me our baby's name – and I feel foolish bringing it up now to anyone else, but maybe it's ok to record it here.

Our baby's name is Tuesday.

It's not a traditional name – but Tuesday is not a traditional child. It was a Tuesday when we found out that our little one had died – and it was the following Tuesday that my body finally let go of the little treasure it wanted so badly to keep. I asked Jack and even though I can tell he thinks I'm crazy, he told me that Tuesday is a lovely name.

Tuesday, September 11th, 2007

Jack signed me up for a writing class. He's so dumb. I told him I'm busy enough with work and I don't want to take a class. He told me it's for my birthday, and I can't reject his birthday gift. My birthday is in July.

Monday, September 17th, 2007

I finally went to the doctor, and when I told her my symptoms (ruptured cyst on my breast, headaches, constant bleeding and a low grade fever) – she sent me for an ultrasound. A few hours later, she phoned me and told me that after consulting with the on call ob-gyn at the hospital, they agreed that I need surgery – tonight.

I'm mad.

She said that my body had retained a part of baby's placenta and that it's too much for my body to take care of on its own. She told me that my cervix is tightly closed and promised me that once I have this surgery, my healing can truly begin. Maybe my exhaustion and my emotional volatility have their root in my body's confused state. I want to weep with frustration. To top it off, Jack's gone this week. His manager is taking him and three other men from the mill to another plant up north to check out a saw they might want to buy. He can't come home... and my doctor firmly believes that I shouldn't wait for him. I feel so rotten; I'm inclined to believe the doctor. I called Megan from work. I just didn't know who else to call at the last minute like this. She said she would be here in an hour to pick me up. I don't know how I'll face her and make small talk. She's always so put together with her shiny black hair cut in a practical short style, and her trendy glasses. Maybe I will just allow myself the luxury of silence and try not to think about what she thinks of me in my helplessness. I always feel like she's rolling her eyes at me, impatient with my slower pace, and my inability to keep up to her as she works harder than ten men.

She sounded sorry for me on the phone though – and she has been has been so understanding towards me these past two months as I have tried so hard to keep it together. She even brought us muffins when we first lost Tuesday. We both love our jobs at the Manor – caring for the residents who live with special needs. It takes a unique kind of individual to want a job like that – and Megan does it masterfully. I have learned so much from her since I started working there two years ago. I just wish I felt like I knew her better – like we had a friendship where we didn't have to try to hide our weaknesses.

I had better go get ready. They want me to come in immediately so they can get me ready even though they can't do the surgery right away because I ate supper.

I wish Jack were here.

Tuesday, September 18th, 2007

So, now... after all this... I am finally, truly empty. Scraped clean by a doctor's knife – all traces of my pregnancy surgically removed from my body. They're testing my blood to make sure that my HCG returns to normal. The doctor said that's the name for the hormone that made my pregnancy test turn positive. He said it had remained elevated, even though I had already miscarried, because of the retained placenta. But now... every trace of Tuesday is gone.

I woke up from surgery sobbing. I felt confused and my throat hurt. It was just after one in the morning. The nurses gave me warmed blankets. They said a doctor would come to see me and that I could probably leave in only a couple more hours. Poor Megan was slumped in a chair sleeping when I woke up next. Her legs were tucked up underneath her and her glasses were propped on the table beside my bed.

And then... there he was, pulling back the curtain and peeking in so carefully. He had a black liquorice cigar in his mouth – and he rattled the box of orange tic-tacs he brought for me with a hopeful smile.

Jack had caught a bus back and took a cab from the bus depot. He got to the hospital in time to take me home. I think Megan was glad; she had to work the next day. I felt bad knowing I cost her a night's sleep, but she was sweet to me and gave me a hug and told me to get better soon. I told her I'll probably see her next week when I'm able to be back at work.

All I wanted was Jack. I didn't want to think, or feel, or talk, or eat. He put me in bed when we got home and sensing my need of him, he climbed in beside me. He was still wearing his dirty work jeans and I was wearing the same sweats I wore to the hospital. He didn't say anything – and neither did I. Why bother– after all, when words would only sully the exchange that we had that night. We slept curled together like two lost children till 7 am when he eased himself out of bed to grab a shower. I pulled the blankets up to my chin – trying to cover more of myself. I felt loopy and tired, but my eyes would only half shut – and sleep refused to return to me. I wanted Jack and it felt like his ten minute shower lasted an eternity.

Before the surgery, I told the doctor that even though I know this is a pretty routine surgery for him, it's not routine for me. He held my hand and told me that he promised to be very careful. I told him that I didn't have any babies yet – and that if ever there was a man who should procreate for the sake of bettering humanity, it's my Jack. He laughed and told me he'd take the very best care, and that he hoped that one day soon Jack and I would make that baby who will change the world.

As I read those words now, I'm left wondering – what is Tuesday's impact?

Little one you lived only 13 short weeks, and yet you've certainly changed my world.

Is it possible that there could be a purpose for that little life, lived in its fragility, only in my womb?

Father? Is it even possible to be a childless mother? I can hardly figure out who I am anymore. And yet, I know that this little baby – barely formed - had substance, and significance – and so too, must I. Were her days numbered for purposes beyond my understanding? Did you measure out the moments of Tuesday's life before she was even conceived?

She.

I don't even get the satisfaction of knowing for certain if Tuesday was a tiny Jack – or a mini Anna.

I smell coffee. It's 9 am and I know Jack has to make an appearance at the mill today. I had better get up and sit with him a bit before he goes and I'm left here alone with my relentless imaginings.

Monday, September 24th, 2007

It has been angry, grey, wet and rainy all week. It's the perfect weather for sitting inside sipping tea in my pajamas with my tears. I took the whole week off work, even though by Thursday I felt better physically than I have for a month. I phoned work on Friday and Megan answered. I told her that I'll be in on Monday and she sounded relieved. She said that Essa has been using her sign for my name constantly. Essa doesn't know very many signs, but she has made up a few for the things and people she loves. I remember the day I realized that when she patted her cheek firmly twice with an open palm, that was her way of saying my name. When she signs Megan, she puts both of her hands on her head and strokes downward. I wonder if that's because of Megan's beautiful shiny hair – or because Megan carefully combs and clips Essa's hair every month whether she needs it or not.

I should have known that Essa would worry about me. She's my little shadow at work.

Right now there are eight residents at The Manor. Every one of them has different needs and different gifts. Each one has challenges that remind me never to take anything for granted, but each one has brought more to the table than they've taken away. Essa is unique because she's non-verbal, and I can't help but love Essa the very best. We're roughly the same age, and especially since I lost Tuesday – her silence has been about the best friendship a person could ask for.

I haven't told her I lost a baby. I didn't even tell her I was pregnant. Megan says that Essa lacks the capacity to understand my situation. She told me to just leave it alone – but when Essa looks at me with that disquiet in her eyes, I can't help but acknowledge that it seems deceitful to keep it from her. I had kind of decided before I went to work this morning that if the right opportunity arose, I'd tell her today.

I got to work - to the familiar din of the breakfast dishes being cleared. I was working the 7-3 shift – getting off in time to get to my first writing class. When I took off my coat and turned around, I found myself wrapped in the warmth of Essa's little arms. Essa has Down syndrome and physically, she's really tiny. She understands every word I speak – and it seems, even more of what I don't speak. She has brown hair cut in the sweetest little bob, thanks to Megan, with perfectly straight bangs framing her gentle face. I noticed that her fingernails were pink and chipped when she took my hand and led me to the couch.

It isn't unusual for Essa to want me all to herself. She likes it when I read to her, or if I'll watch a movie with her, or we paint each other's nails. Essa loves fabrics and she is in charge of tying up all the rag quilts that they sell at the market. She is never without a fresh stack of fabrics that she'll constantly be fingering as she picks out the new patterns and colors for a new batch of quilts. She'll often drag me over to the couch to show me the pieces that she has put together to see how they'll look once they've been stitched. This time, she didn't have her bag of fabrics with her, and she was strangely somber as she pushed me down and sat down next to me.

I smiled at her and was about to ask her what we were going to be doing today when something about the way she was looking at me made me stop.

She looked fixedly at me with those almond eyes – and I wished for the millionth time that she could speak. I read in her file that she used to have some limited speech, but that she had quit speaking after her last stint in foster care before coming permanently to the Manor. It makes me ache for her to know that someone, or something - circumstances I'll never know or understand, took that away from her.

She sat down beside me – and there was fire in her eyes as she held my gaze. Her short, broad hands reached for me and she laid her brown head on my shoulder. She reached up with her face hidden from me and placed her hand on my cheek and pressed it once... twice.

It was like she was whispering my name.

I closed my eyes, suddenly feeling the tension creep from my bones, and let out my breath. I felt I was safe, in the presence of a trusted confidant.

Without warning, she pulled her little hand from mine and so gently laid it on my stomach.

My heart turned to ice and in my staggering shock, I was too surprised to move.

She started rocking – and making crooning, weeping noises as she pressed her tiny self against me. Suddenly, I was too hot. I was overcome... overcome with the sadness I had been carrying. My chest started heaving, and my little friend became like a mother to me. She soothed my distress and eased the anguish of my loss – her low moan, a lament as she held me in her capable arms. She smoothed my hair and straightened my disheveled sleeves. Her sigh was like a prayer as she released her breath slowly, patiently and held me while I wept. When finally I pulled myself from her, she smiled her impish smile and stood to leave.

She knew.

I have no doubt she knew. Her impish smile was bravado; I had seen the sorrow in her eyes as she so gently took me where I had been afraid to go.

Then Megan came around the corner and told me that breakfast was cleared up and she was finished her shift and ready to go home.

By the time we were done talking, Essa had already slipped away to another corner of the house where she was working on some baskets for the farmer's market, and I didn't get a chance to talk to her – or thank her – for grieving with me.

Friday, September 28th, 2007

I didn't feel like writing anymore this week. It feels too morose to write in a pregnancy journal. Jack feels bad for buying it for me right before I ended up needing the surgery. He told me even if the noise is the quieter scratching of pen on paper, he's glad I'm making noise again.

I went to my writing class on Monday. Right on the heels of Essa's love, I felt safe going. I actually contemplated bringing Essa with me. She loves outings, and I was sure she would enjoy a classroom setting, but in the end I just went on my own. I thought it might be better for me to get comfortable there on my own, and make sure it would be a good place to bring Essa before showing up with her unannounced.

The class is not really a class; it's just a community program with five people registered including me. The learning outcomes include, "an ability to express thoughts, ideas and emotions in a written format". It sounded like something even I couldn't mess up.

The instructor is Henry Dyck, a retired junior high language arts teacher. I felt a little ridiculous showing up, not knowing what to expect, with my pen and paper, dictionary and thesaurus – which were the only requirements of the class. There were two high school students whose teachers had recommended they take the class so they have a better chance of graduating in the spring who were sitting in the back, looking just as uncomfortable as I felt. There's also a woman who is about 45 or so who said she has always wanted to learn how to write to express herself more thoughtfully. She had an electronic thesaurus and dictionary and a bright pink coil bound book to write in. Of course after me, that only leaves the older man who sat in the back writing slowly, methodically on his scrap paper as Mr. Henry talked. He said he was taking the class as a favor to his wife. She had been begging him to write some sort of family history for their children and he said he felt a little nervous getting started. When we went around the room giving our introductions, he seemed kind of embarrassed, so I jumped in and told them that I was there for my husband, just like he was there for his wife. I told them that we didn't have a family – or even very much history yet to speak of... but I hoped that one day, I would share his reasons for needing to learn how to write.

Mr. Henry is not at all what I expected. He's really quiet – and he told us that he would try to give us assignments that would help us meet our individual goals. He said that our first assignment would be to choose a word – it can be any word - and think of a time when we experienced that word in a unique way. He gave us an example with the word balloon. He said that over the summer he had the opportunity to ride in a hot air balloon for the first time – he said that the word balloon now brought to mind the image of billowing fabric, the heave of the breeze – the rippling tearing sound as the balloon filled and the anticipation that swelled as the belly of the balloon filled.

When I got home, I chose my word; vigil – from the Latin word vigilia which means 'wakefulness'. The online dictionaries defined the word vigil as a period of sleeplessness, an occasion for devotional watching or observance. And then I wrote for the first time about that week I spent – knowing my baby had died inside me – carrying her – knowing she was already gone. It felt so good to write it down. It felt good to say, 'this is what happened'. It felt right to acknowledge the week that showed me how to mother a dead child – to honor her life and The One who gave that life, in its brevity, to me.

A Miscarriage Vigil

God, keep me grateful.
Show me how to live my life - in these days - with gratitude.
Help me see Your Purpose.
I know you've got me here for a reason.
I know you haven't forgotten me here.
These days, I've been thinking that physical pain would just be
so much better.
Is it that I'm not willing to let go?
I'm trying to.
Every morning I wake up to realize that I'm still here.
Every morning my heart breaks again,
as I realize my body isn't nourishing and growing this child.
My body is carrying the little body that you knit together in the
secret place...
And sometimes I feel like the load is too heavy...
like I might break under the weight of it.
Oh, but God,
in these walls,
I've felt you here.
I've felt the warmth and peace that your presence brings.
I've felt you drawing me in.
I've felt you holding, carrying, and lifting me.
I will praise you when I wake in the morning,
I will praise you for your faithfulness,
I will praise you in the evenings- when sleep won't come- and
my mind won't stop.
I will make a choice to praise you.
I praise you through the tears;
I praise you through the pain.
I know you've taken what I've lost
and saved what I could not...
I praise you in the present
because I know you hold the future.

Tuesday, October 30th, 2007

I should be 31 weeks pregnant. I know because when I found out I was pregnant, I wrote every single week on my calendar—right up to my "due date". I remember Jack was excited our baby was due on New Year's Day. He said it would be good for our son in sports if his birthday landed so soon in the New Year. I reminded him that it was entirely possible that our sporty son could be a sporty daughter, or a non-sporty son, or an early baby, arriving in time for Christmas. I didn't ever dream that long before Christmas, I would find myself in such a desolate place.

I haven't been able to bring myself to write these past weeks. Work has been busy – and my silly writing class has become a bit of an obsession. He had us writing poetry last week – and my every attempt was a miserable failure. Poetry is broken in me. Words are useless blocks; they're totally incapable of capturing the intricacies of my grief. I sit in my class while Mr. Henry reads to us – and has us copy the work of the greatest poets and writers who have ever lived, and I find myself completely overwhelmed with my inadequacy.

I tried to write a sonnet – about my weakened ability to talk to Jack. Conversations are stolen whispers in the night – little phrases, "I'm sad." Followed by his, "I know."

The aching failure seething between us seems silenced somehow by Jack's sure steady heartbeat – and I let the tears fall on his chest as we lie in the dark and I listen to it thump in my ear...

In Secret

Alive, my secrets whisper'd in the dark;
I note with breakneck speed, my beating heart;
stops mid step - unsure - and in his face mark;
what feeling lies therein? Words stop... then start.

My secret swells and contracts between us;
Like a beating heart - no longer contained;

I lie still - (inside all's writhing, anxious)-
and wish fervently that she were still chained.

What obstacle would try to hold love back?
What worthy foe could ambush us and win?
Her pow'r when unspoken in inky black
dissipates now, becoming weak and thin.

Secrets crip'ling blow can only love cure;
at home where hearts are of each other sure.

Thursday, November 1st, 2007

I realized today that it has been over six weeks since my surgery – and I began to wonder why things haven't returned to normal like they should. I have been half dreading, half hoping for the beginning of normalcy again, but a seedling of doubt started in my mind when I was at work and so I stopped by the drug store on the way home and bought a two pack pregnancy test.

Jack is working nights this week and he wasn't home, so there was nobody here to whisper words of caution reminding me how quickly heartbreak arrives. Jack would have warned me not to hope so hard. Not that I would have listened anyway.

I took the test.

Baby, I'm sure I see just the faintest line.

This kind of poetry requires no words – it's seeping from my pores, and puddling on the ground around my feet. If I could capture it now in a rondeau or a sestina – even the unpennable sonnet – I would have something precious. This is poetry – the beauty of life intertwining with the poignancy of sorrow and the hope of love.

Tomorrow, I'll sober up and remember morning sickness. Tomorrow, I'll worry. Tomorrow, I'll tell Jack. Today is the day I found out I'm getting another chance.

Friday, November 2nd, 2007

Jack got home at 7 am. I met him at the door with my pregnancy test and all he did was grab my wrists to keep it out of his face while laughing, 'EWWWWW, you PEED on that!' I thought we were going to wake the neighbors. He said he knew I was pregnant all along and then he went straight to sleep; typical Jack. I tried to harass him for awhile, but he would have none of it and since I know he has another night shift tonight, I decided to let him be. I don't have to work until three today so maybe when my heart quits pounding, I'll go climb into bed with him and make up for a restless night last night.

Later –

Work was awful. I walked around like I was in a daze half the day. I spilled hot coffee right beside Tina and it surprised us both, I squealed and it scared her so bad it made her cry. Thank goodness she wasn't hurt! I think Megan was frustrated with my clumsiness. We were both kind of on edge too because Essa has a cold and it's sounding so bad I almost wonder if she has pneumonia – poor girl can't catch a break. Megan says she has a doctor's appointment set up for her tomorrow. Megan seemed kind of 'off' too. I think she just wanted to get home because her husband is leaving for a month long stint in the oil rigs on Monday. She has three teenagers at home needing her too. Finally, at around ten I told her she should just leave, that I would cover for her since everyone was already in bed anyway and there wasn't anything else to get done. I could tell she didn't want to, but there really wasn't any more work to be done. She thanked me and said she owed me – which we both know she doesn't – and ran for her car. Once she left, it felt like such a relief to be alone with my thoughts.

I guess I'll need to phone a doctor or something. Jack and I toyed with the idea of a midwife last time. I wonder if that would be a good thing – just to make everything different this time, rather than going to the same office and seeing the same doctor... bringing up the worry of walking down that same long tunnel of grief again. I'll ask Jack when he gets home. I'm glad it's his last night shift and we'll get the rest of the weekend off together.

Saturday, November 3rd, 2007

Finally I got a full night's sleep. We slept in until noon, and I feel restored. Jack claims he's fine with the five hours he got since he only got home at seven in the morning, but his red rimmed eyes are ratting him out. He has had three strong cups of coffee so far and his hair is sticking up all over the place like it always does before he has a shower. He's wearing his horrible cut off sweat pants with the paint all over them and his slippers with the hole in the toe. He looks like he'll only be good for another hour or two before he needs to visit the land of Wynken, Blynken and Nod. When he sleeps, it is such a peaceful, deep sleep. His lashes are so thick they seem to weigh down his lids and I wonder how he manages to open them come morning. I'm grateful, though, that he got up with me so we can face the day together.

I talked to him about the possibility of a midwife and he said it was up to me. I did an online search for midwives in our area and I found there is one practice. I'm surprised and thankful; since we live in a pretty small town I haven't ever heard of anyone who has used a midwife here. I sent them an email giving as many details as I've got and I'm hoping they'll get back to me soon.

I wonder when this buzz will end. Already, I feel the beginnings of nagging worry as I wonder if my body will fail us all again – or if by some miracle this will all end when it should in nine months time – with a beautiful beginning. The only comforting thing is that I know that it's out of my hands. I can take my B vitamins, my prenatal supplement, get my rest and exercise. I can read every pregnancy book and magazine – pouring over statistics and websites. I can make sure to stay away from soft cheeses and sushi and get the recommended daily amount of protein. I can cry, weep, moan and beg – to keep what is not mine to begin with.

Or I can surrender.

I guess the question I keep coming back to over these past sorrowful months is the same question we all have to ask ourselves at some point in our lives. Is God good? Assuming we even believe in God in the first place. These days, I find myself in the deepest most intimate places of my soul knowing that He's there, but asking myself if He's trustworthy.

And I guess the conclusion I'm coming to is yes.

Yes, God is good.

In the silence of grief and the loneliness of failure – I have felt him in the room, watching me long for Him. The ties that bind me to heaven have been strengthened since Tuesday went there before me. Death is real and tangible. Heaven is equally real – and yet invisible and complicated and hard to understand.

Mr. Henry gave us a new assignment for our writing class. He told me that my style of writing – which I have always thought of as a hot mess – is called 'poetic prose'. He said that writing can be therapeutic and he told me I should feel free to write what's in my mind, heart and life without the fear of failure – or even the fear of having to share it with him or the class. Our new assignment is to think of a regular routine that I take part in, and tear it down into smaller bite sized pieces. He used as his example making the perfect cup of coffee. We looked for all the aspects that make that cup of coffee perfect. What steps did we go through to make it – and why does this ritual become a part of our routine?

I think I might write about church.

Our church is far from perfect, but the ritual of going to that little brick building week after week has sure become a part of our routine. Losing Tuesday has made me look past the shell of ritual to the kernel of truth. Maybe I can explain it in my bumbling 'prose' as Mr. Henry puts it.

Jack's waiting for me. He said he can't last another weekend away from the water and rocks and ruggedness, so we're going for a hike. There's a little canyon that's only about an hour's drive from our house. We have had a sudden reprieve from the aching cold that has been holding us captive lately and it will feel good to be outside these walls that can tend to trap me if I let them. He says if I don't come right now, he's going back to bed and judging from the red rims of his eyes, he's not bluffing. I'm sure he'll crash hard when we get home.

This Is the Church I Go To

Hey, let me introduce us...

We're the broken - the sick - the lost - the dying...

We've struggled with death and disease, some of us have come here looking for answers, not knowing if we believe in heaven at all... some have become hard and calloused and don't even know why we're here Sunday after Sunday. Still others of us come because we need fellowship with other people who love Jesus...

Some of us are struggling with infertility, some of us have been cheated on, disrespected, abandoned by spouses who should have known better. Some of us have been happily married for decades. Some of us are lonely, guilty, shy, boisterous, bitter or happy. Some of us are reeling from circumstances that have spiraled far beyond our control.

This is the church that I go to.

Some of us mouth the words of the songs because our hearts would break if we *really* sang those words. Some of us are unemployed, former addicts, present day mess-ups, control-freaks or successful businessmen. Some of us are grieving our babies lost to miscarriage - others grieving our children lost to abortion - and still others are gratefully anticipating new life with swelling bellies and tearful gratitude.

This is the church I go to.

Our childhoods are as varied as the rest of our lives. Some were happy, some of us were neglected, abused, ignored, or abandoned. Some of us were motherless, others fatherless - some of us got good grades and some of us are drop outs. Some of us still feel stuck in those years - the hurts won't heal and we come here looking for answers... looking for *Jesus*... so we can quit wasting away and start living.

This is the church I go to.

Some of us come straight from work, others from hellish, unimaginable situations, and some straight from a good night's rest. Some of us go home to empty houses, or warm lunches, or out to work again...

But on Sunday morning, we gather as a congregation. We, who are daily becoming aware of our need,

Jesus,
He is the cup - and we are thirsty - parched, crawling and almost delirious with our need.

Jesus.
He is the bread - our frail bodies are wracked with hunger.

Jesus.
We're clinging to the cross...

This is the church I go to.

On hearing this, Jesus said, "It is not the healthy who need a doctor, but the sick. But go and learn what this means: 'I desire mercy, not sacrifice.' For I have not come to call the righteous, but sinners." Matthew 9:12-13

Tuesday, November 6th, 2007

The midwife called me back yesterday! She said she would love to take us on and booked us an appointment for next Tuesday. She said she's in a practice with three other midwives and their offices are in a little house that they converted into a birthing center. I didn't even know it existed!

It's only about three blocks away from The Manor, so that will sure make things easy. Jack rearranged things at work so that he'll be able to make it to my first appointment.

I know Jack's little brother, Aaron was born with a midwife at home shortly after his parents moved back to Australia. I think it was mostly because a midwife was more readily available in their out of the way location. I'll have to ask his mom next time she calls. I wish they lived closer – and my mom and dad too.

It is fun being stout hearted little pilgrims on our own trail of life, but at times like these, I ache for our family. But then I remember that Jack's mom had four healthy boys, and my mom just had me and my sister – neither one of them ever lost a baby, and I figure that they wouldn't understand anyway. I guess when I think about it, I haven't really given either of them the chance though. Maybe I shouldn't be so very selfish with my sorrow.

I feel like I'm a wild animal with a festering wound. The rational part of me acknowledges that those I love aren't going to poke at and hurt me where they know I'm tender – and yet there's this over riding primal urge to protect my vulnerability. It seems impossible for me to balance the two forces at work within me.

On the note of vulnerability, I ran into Mr. Henry at the grocery store. He took my hand and whispered in my ear, "I guess you and I must go to the same church then." Then he smiled and winked at me and walked away. Jack was with me and he asked me what Mr. Henry had said. I told him it was just about some noise I had made in my writing class.

Tuesday November 13th, 2007

We had our first midwife appointment today. I wish I could describe in intricate detail, the look on Jack's face when we walked in there.

The walls are painted deep shades of purple – and the window coverings are made of silk scarves – also in varying shades of violet, lilac and plum. The scarves swoop across the room – draped from silver hooks in the ceiling and tied with twine. The house was built in the 50's and still has a lot of the original features. It has gleaming hardwood floors and an old gas stove in the kitchen, with the original bright blue arborite counters. The furnishings are all new and modern though – with a flat screen television, internet access, big plush couches and a la-z-boy recliner. I thought it was the perfect blend of simplicity and comfort, of vintage charm and organic ease. There were three birthing rooms, all outfitted with modern medical equipment, should the need arise. Each bedroom has an enormous ensuite. The one that we saw had a deep tub and a tile floor that slanted to the drain in the middle. In the corner was a shower with a removable shower head and no walls. There is a stereo system in each room, and dimmers on every light switch. The bed is a king size, with lots of pillows and a cozy looking comforter.

Then I turned and my heart skipped a beat. I don't know why it should have been such a shock to me to see a tiny wooden bassinet in the corner of the room, waiting, and empty. I felt my stomach lurch, half in mourning, and half in hope. Visual reminders of what I have lost confuse me when they're in the context of what we're going to become.

The basement is a walk out, and I noticed they had a play area for older siblings and offices for the midwives who practice there. The art work though, is what completely floored Jack. Whimsical, **hippy** pregnant bellies painted with **psychedelic** shapes and patterns - floating pregnant bodies with enormous bare breasts - some modern version of a mythical gestational dreamland. When we first saw them, I couldn't help turning to look at him, my eyes dancing, daring him to comment. He said nothing, just cleared his throat and reached over squeezing my hand while muttering, "Lovely, just breathtaking..." with a completely straight face, until I was completely undone. The contrast of my six foot tall husband in his steel toed boots and thick plaid work jacket pretending to admire the swirling womanly art on the purple walls of this house struck me funny. Jack continued to marvel at the artwork – trying get me to laugh out loud. The midwife walked ahead of us and she either ignored or failed to perceive his jovial teasing tone and responded to his quips with, "Yes, it sure is – the artist has several prints available for purchase..." I thought I was going to explode.

My midwife, Sam, took us to the living room to have our first meeting. On our way there, she offered us a cup of tea and told us we were lucky there were no births happening at the moment, so we had the house to ourselves. As soon as we were settled, she went through our history.

When I told her that I lost our first baby, she stopped me and told me how very sorry she was. I didn't feel like I could even talk about it anymore than telling her the medical facts of what had happened, and even so, I couldn't stop my hot tears from flowing. She asked if I wanted to get an early ultrasound – partly for dating purposes since I had never cycled between my surgery and this newest pregnancy – and partly just for our peace of mind. Jack spoke for us, interrupting her, and told her we did. She said she would set that up in the next week or so. We spent a good hour with her – talking about our little family, and what we could expect from using a midwife for our prenatal care.

When we left, Jack was grinning wickedly the minute we were out of earshot and asked me if maybe we should purchase some of the artwork for our front room. I told him I liked it and I would love some of it for my birthday present and that really, I was pleasantly surprised by his sublime taste. He reminded me that I already got my birthday present and if I really loved him, I would make some more scratching noise with my pen on paper; because that's the kind of artwork he likes the best.

So that's what I did.

Monday, November 19th, 2007

Sam called today and said she booked us an ultrasound for this Thursday, the 22nd! It couldn't have worked out better with our work schedules. I'm so glad Jack didn't have to rearrange yet another work day because of me.

We never had an ultrasound with Tuesday until I had a little bit of spotting and they couldn't find a heartbeat with the Doppler. Even so, we were sure nothing was wrong since it was so early yet. The doctor recommended an ultrasound just to make sure things were progressing as they should.

Of course, they weren't... and now, my only memory of ultrasound is of the silence in the room, the painful waiting as I thought my bladder would explode and Jack's horrible, ragged exhalation as the doctor said, "I'm so sorry. There is a foetus, measuring at about thirteen weeks gestation, but no heartbeat."

I don't even remember anything after that – what he said, what we did.

Oh, God, let us see life at this ultrasound.

Tuesday, November 20th, 2007

Essa was admitted to the hospital today. They were worried about the possible strain the pneumonia could have on her heart. I want to go see her, but when I phoned the hospital, they said she has been sleeping a lot and that maybe later on in the week would be better for a visit. I double checked that they were continuing her thyroid medication and the doctor laughed at me and assured me he knew what he was doing.

Sometimes I worry though, that in her silence, Essa will be overlooked. I have never met her biological parents and I have no idea if she has any family to speak of. I feel like if I don't speak for her, who will? She has lived in dangerous, shameful situations since she was a tiny, vulnerable baby. She was a Crown Ward when she was 2 weeks old, a full 2 months before she should have even been born, since she came so early. She survived abuse and neglect, along with open heart surgery and the loss of spoken words – and it makes me ashamed for humanity that we couldn't have done better when someone as stunning as Essa was born, and needed us. How arrogant we've become when we're unwilling to respond to the neediness of the vulnerable – because we're blind to our own need for compassion, goodness and mercy.

Thursday, November 22nd, 2007

We heard a precious heart, beating at 165 beats per minute. Our little one is measuring at exactly 7 weeks, giving us a due date of July tenth.

When the technician left the room, Jack murmured, "Who knew all that comforting would be so fruitful?" and he gave me a cocky grin. I recognized the relief in his voice when he grabbed my hair and whispered kind of fiercely in my ear, "We're gonna have a little baby, Anna."

I think I believe him.

Thursday, November 29th, 2007

I'm eight weeks pregnant. I stepped on the scale today to see if I have gained any weight and it looks like I've already put on a couple of pounds. The day after my ultrasound, I started throwing up and the only thing that seems to help is eating – so I have been eating constantly for the past week. I think maybe Jack felt bad for me at first, but by Monday, he was over it. I wish I could be over it! On Tuesday, I was throwing up in our bathroom after he had worked a night shift – he called out from bed, "Hey, Anna, I feel bad for you and everything, but some of us are trying to sleep over here."

I'm glad one of us still has a sense of humor. I can't believe I have been so sick and still managed to pack on a couple of pounds. At this rate, I don't think we'll be able to keep our tiny one a secret for long.

If this is to be a true record of pregnancy, I guess I should be honest and tell you that in the midst of the morning sickness, I'm finding it impossible to wipe this incessant smile off my face. And yet, added to the nausea and the feeling of elation, there is another constant companion. I have been having a hard time with fear lately. I have been trying desperately not to fall in love, all the while falling harder and harder. The morning sickness is no comfort. I felt exactly this same way with Tuesday.

The thing I find hardest to accept is that everything can be fine – until it's not. Everything can progress normally until all of a sudden, your baby dies. Why? Did I drink coffee? Did I have too much vitamin A? Was there a chromosomal issue that made it impossible for our little one to thrive?

How do I learn to hold this baby with open hands, allowing Him to give... and to take? I have five more weeks until I pass the week that Tuesday died. I have to make it through five more weeks of perpetual worry and relentless self doubt. At times it seems too cruel that there is nothing else I can do to ensure that my little one lives. I find myself researching endlessly on the internet about progesterone creams, blood thinner injections, bed rest, or the cure all supplement. Our midwife felt that there wasn't a good enough reason to pursue any of these extra regimens yet, other than a healthy diet and reasonable care. Part of me wants to scream at her to DO SOMETHING because this is a life and death situation, while another part of me whispers that all is really well, and that I should let this little one grow in peace.

Friday, November 30th, 2007

Finally, it's the last day of November. I don't know why I feel like that brings me that much closer to my baby, but it does.

Essa is still in the hospital. It has been ten days and when I went to see her, I could tell that it has been ten very long days for her. The doctors say that she's having trouble keeping food down now too. I don't understand how that's connected to her pneumonia. She's having such a hard time kicking it. I crawled into bed beside her when I saw her lying so wee and fragile – her skin looking almost as white as those hospital sheets. She wrapped her arms around my neck and I noticed that she had on a new shade of orange chipped nail polish. I'll have to remember to bring a new color with me the next time I go.

She's so little.

I know I should be careful with the baby and I should try not to get sick, but Essa just clung to me. She cuddled up to the warmth of my body like she just needed to be held. I stayed with her till she fell asleep, singing in her ear and smoothing down her perfect little bob haircut. I feel like that's the least I could do for her, seeing how much she has done for me.

Sunday, December 2nd, 2007

Each morning brings another day, another worry, another insane Anna trying to control the spin of the universe.

God, I'm done. I'm done. I'm laying it all down. No more articles about average miscarriage rates, signs of missed miscarriage, or undiagnosed ectopic pregnancy. I'm done. This baby's life is in your hands – my life too for that matter. I love you. I feel peace just now coming to you and laying it all down again.

I went to bed last night with a headache and woke up with a headache and nausea this morning. I went back to bed by nine in the morning and now it's three in the afternoon, and I'm still in bed.

And I'm still smiling.

I'll take sickness over anxiety any day of the week. I have started to ask God for peace, rather than a healthy baby.

Monday, December 3rd, 2007

I had my writing class yesterday. Les showed the class the folder that he has been working on for his family history. It's really a thing of beauty. His wife has saved pictures and documented each of their 46 years of marriage. They have 10 children, and 46 grandchildren – one for every single year they've been married. Les writes slowly and thoughtfully. I can see now why his wife wanted the memoir to be in his words. His eloquence and gentle humor are worth the wait as he laboriously puts together what will be an amazing keepsake in years to come. It somehow made me a little less afraid to tell bits and pieces of my own story; to share the agony of losing Tuesday, and the joy in being given a second chance.

I can bare my soul for the sake of my children, can't I?

Tuesday, December 4th, 2007

I phoned Mom today and told her I'm pregnant again. She was smiling. I could hear it in her voice. She called Dad and got him on the phone too – and they gave me every bit of the reaction I was looking for. I asked her to keep it quiet for just a bit longer. The fewer people that know, the more I am forced to bring all my anxiety to God – and In His presence I find it easier to find the peace that I am so desperate for.

Mom told me that it takes a leap of faith to have one baby, and then it takes that same leap to choose to have another. I told her that for me – I feel like God is saying, "Hey, Anna, hold still a minute. I may or may not hit you with this baseball bat – but I'm gonna have to ask you not to flinch." There's something in seeing God like that that seems unkind; or lacking in compassion. Both of those things I know are not true of Him.

Mom said maybe we're trying to humanize God too much - that we're trying to make human sense out of Someone who is so much more than human.

I feel like I can dig in where it hurts and try to know Him more, or I can give a pat answer and gloss over the things that don't make sense to me.

Mom has always said, "Without truth, there can be no relationship". I'm realizing now, how much there is that I don't know or understand about God. I can't avoid seeking truth, if my goal is to have relationship.

We phoned Jack's parents too. We always have such a hard time figuring out when to phone them because of the 15 hour time difference. We decided to just phone at 8 pm and take the chance that they would be around since that would make it 11 am there. Jack talked to his dad first; I love how he gets just the tiniest bit of an accent when they talk. Jack was born in Canada, but lived in Australia for five years when he was a teenager. His mom is Canadian and his dad grew up not too far from the city of Darwin, Australia in a smaller mining community. They met when she decided to take her schooling all the way around the world, just for the adventure of it all. When they came back to Canada to get married, they didn't end up leaving for 15 years.

Jack told me that one day when he was about 12, his parents called him and his brothers in for a family meeting. They asked them what they'd think of moving back to Australia. Of course, being adventurous little boys, they were beyond excited. Jack said before they moved back, he had only been to Darwin once – for his grandmother's funeral – and he and his brothers bragged how they would visit the outback and tame a kangaroo for a pet.

Jack's dad ended up getting a job at the mine in the community where he grew up, and they packed up their family and made the huge journey back.

Jack's mom told me that her mother never forgave her for moving that far away. I don't blame her. My parents are only 10 hours away and it feels like we never get to see them. I can't imagine how hard it would be to send your daughter and her whole family half way around the world, knowing how few and far between the opportunities would come for face to face visits.

Jack's three brothers all still live in Australia. Two of them are schooling away from home but his youngest brother is still in high school and living at home.

My Jack though, decided to come to Canada and live with his grandparents for a year after he graduated high school. His grandparents lived only four blocks away from our family, and they attended the same church we went to at the time. I still remember Jack showing up at church, with his short hair sticking up like he had just rolled out of bed and his eyes... his eyes were only for me. He was wearing grungy jeans and an un-tucked flannel shirt over a pristine white T-shirt. He wasn't gregarious or outgoing; he was quiet with a wry sense of humor. He made me sit up and take notice – with his subdued disposition.

We ended up hanging out quite a bit that year. We were both busy – I was taking the care aide course at our community college, and Jack was working and going to school in an apprenticeship program for his millwright ticket. But we found time, stretching out the days far into the evening and even waking early to meet for coffee on the days we had morning classes. Sleep was a casualty of our budding alliance, and as far as I was concerned, it was a worthy sacrifice.

At the end of the year, Jack went home. I remember feeling confused at my own hurt. Wondering why he left; why he didn't see what I saw. Whenever he had walked into a room, his brown eyes would look for me, slowly spanning the room till they found me – and I felt sure that this feeling – of being 'found' – wasn't something to take lightly.

He finally wrote me a letter and it was terrible, of course. Just a note really, that in his scrawled handwriting told me what television show he had watched and that he was having a hard time transferring over his schooling to his new program. That tiny bit of access was all I needed – his innocent letter invited a barrage of words, penned in black felt tip – and sent in brightly colored envelopes. For every five letters I sent, Jack would send back one. We sent emails too, and the occasional awkward phone call – but it was our paper letters that changed everything. It was on a paper letter that he finally wrote that he loved me. I knew it already. That was the whole reason I couldn't let Jack get away. His love is constant, unflappable and steady. My love is stormy, passionate and unpredictable. I knew that my fervent heart would never love another man like I loved Jack, and that if he was willing to let me in on the ceaseless well of his love too, then we were going to have something amazing. And we do.

Jack talked to his dad for what seemed like forever before he broke the news, and at the word "pregnant", I heard their cheers as Jack pulled the phone away from his ear. His parents were so excited, and they wanted to know every detail; how I had been feeling, when was the due date, did it look like everything was going well this time?

Aside from Tuesday, this little baby will be the first grandchild in both our families. I think they have all been holding their breath, not daring to say a word, but hoping that soon, we would find solace in the hope of another baby. Jack was laughing and his accent was getting thicker all the time, and then after a bit, he handed me the phone. He said his mom wanted to talk to me.

I have always liked Jack's mom. Even though I have only met her in person four times, she emails me every single week, and she's always so warm and steady – just like my Jack.

"Congratulations, Anna!" She said, and before I could respond she quickly added, "I want to pray for you."

She paused, and I thought she meant she was going to be praying for me during my pregnancy. I was grateful and I started to tell her how much her prayers would be appreciated, but then she really started to pray. Right there on the phone. I felt my legs give way beneath me as I crumpled to the couch and her warm voice continued over the phone. The tears streamed down my face as I held the phone up to my ear and listened to the words of blessing flow from the other side of the world, penetrating my clichéd expectation of a trite offer to pray, with the sincerity of a saint who knew the Father well enough to storm His throne on my behalf.

Baby, I wish I could have recorded your grandmother's prayer for you. She covered us in blessing, praising God for the miracle of your tender life. She prayed for me and your daddy, for us to have peace and strength and patience to wait as you grow. She prayed that you would, even now, have a tiny heart that longs to please God and that you would grow in wisdom and stature and favor with God and man. And with just the slightest quake in her voice, she prayed for you to live.

Tuesday December 11th, 2007

I had my second midwife appointment today. She got me to weigh myself and then we went to her office in the basement because there was a family using the birthing center. I could hear the creak of the floor as people walked back and forth above us. The pipes banged and hummed as water ran and I felt like an intruder as I listened to the preparations being made above. My midwife smiled as she caught me staring at the ceiling. She said that the young mother upstairs had been laboring for 14 hours. It was her third baby and she was tired. She hoped that soon, the work would be finished and that she would be rewarded for her efforts. I hoped so too, as I heard a cry of pain float down the vents to where we sat in the offices below.

Then she leaned down, putting her elbows on her knees and asked about me. She asked how I have been feeling. I was honest with her about the constant struggle with fear. I told her that I feel the perfect blend of anxiety and joy – perpetually. She told me that it's hard because fear is often exacerbated by hormonal fluctuations. She encouraged me to keep taking my B vitamins, and to exercise. She seemed to think that I'll probably start feeling a little more confident when I'm feeling a little less sick, and a lot more pregnant. I sure hope she's right. It's strange how my anxiety and joy seem to coexist. I would have thought that one would diminish the power of the other, but it seems the opposite is true. The anxiety just reminds me of my gratitude, and my joy reminds me of the potential for loss. I'm constantly vacillating between the two – often experiencing both in the same sigh.

Afterwards, I went to get some groceries. It has been bitterly cold. Fall came early and has seemed so clumsy and insolent. We had already had heavy snowfall twice before the end of September. I forgot to bring my winter jacket with me and the cold pricked my fingers as I pushed the cart through the slush to get to the front door. I couldn't believe all the Christmas decorations up everywhere. It's funny, I'll be in the most random place at the most random moment and feel the most bewildering melancholy – and then I'll realize – I should have hit this or that milestone of pregnancy. I should be buying maternity clothes, not ice-chips and soda crackers. It's almost Christmas and I should be finishing up my pregnancy – not loitering near the end of my first trimester.

When I drove home, I drove past the birthing center and they had blue balloons in the window, with a sign out front, "It's a boy!"

It was kind of incredible. And so, so sweet; I can't wait till we get the chance to announce our little one's arrival in the same way.

Monday, December 17th, 2007

Megan and I were working on the schedule today. I offered to work both Christmas and New Years. Jack is scheduled to work them too this year, so I figured we might as well both work and take a holiday either before or after Christmas. Megan couldn't believe I didn't mind working both of them, but I told her; really, she's doing us a favor because we could sure use the time and a half. I didn't tell her about our new baby coming in the summer – I figured there is plenty of time for that after the craziness of the holidays have passed.

She said that her husband Cam was going to be home for Christmas this year and that since the kids had a nice long break for the holidays, they were thinking that if she could get off work it would be nice to go visit some of her family up north. She hemmed and hawed for awhile about whether or not she should let me take them both while I continued to assure her that it wasn't a big deal and that it would be better to be at the Manor than alone at home while Jack was at the mill.

I wish I knew Megan better. She's so abrupt and adept. She works harder than anyone else at the Manor – actually, she works harder than anyone else I know. She always seems to know just what to do no matter what ridiculous situation we find ourselves in, and at the Manor, there is no shortage of ridiculous situations. She does all the grocery shopping for the Manor and makes sure that the meals taste good and are healthy too. She gets after me if I let Tina get away with eating no vegetables at all. And the reason I know there is more to Megan than she lets on is because I know it was Megan who went to battle with social services to let Essa come live at the Manor, even though she was only 16 and the social worker thought she should stay in foster care for another year.

Megan told me once on a late night with rare openness how she had met Essa when Essa was only 15 and she would occasionally come to work the odd shift at the Workshop. She said she had a gut feeling that something wasn't right at home, and was uneasy enough to decide to stop in unannounced at the place she was living. Within minutes of walking through the front door, she said she knew that this home was a dangerous place. She wouldn't elaborate on what she had seen, but she said she told the foster family that she wasn't leaving without Essa. They let her go. She took Essa with her to the social worker's office that very night and filed a complaint against the foster father. Megan doesn't like to talk about it, and obviously Essa hasn't told me anything either; there isn't too much information on her file and I know that even now, there are still legal matters that are being processed regarding Essa's foster care, and the vile man who collected a paycheque for keeping Essa in his home. Megan brushed me off when I asked about getting Essa in to see a counselor; or even a speech therapist. She said Essa just needed to pick herself up and brush herself off. I wish she would have a little more softness and a little less perfection. I wish she would let me in to that whirling dervish of activity she calls her life – and let her guard down for just a minute so I could get to know the woman inside.

Finally, she relented and scrawled my name down for both holidays with curt thanks.

Scheduling aside, it was one of those head shaking days at work. Everyone seemed to be a little out of sorts. If you've ever been to the Manor, it looks massive, but really it's not, it's just that the Workshop is attached to it. While no men live at the Manor, there are a few who come to work at the Workshop every day. They make all kinds of gorgeous arts and crafts for the Farmer's Market. Out of our eight residents, seven of them work at the Workshop, everyone except for Nikki. Nikki loves her job at the coffee shop and she feels pretty important when her dad comes to pick her up every morning for work. He always bursts in and swoops her up in his arms. Then he asks her if she's ready to work hard. She always gives a big sigh and puts on a big show turning to me with the biggest grin on her face, "My dad's here. My dad is taking me to work now. I need to go with my dad to get to work. I'll come home after I'm done work with my dad. My dad will bring me home." And he smiles like he's the proudest man in the whole world. Sometimes if he can't pick her up, one of her older brothers comes for her instead. They treat her just the same way he does, and they tease her about fending off her boyfriends. I love that family.

Anyway, back to today. Essa has been back at the Manor for a week now, but she's still pretty weak and is just not herself yet. She was wearing her slippers at the Workshop when something or other happened and she got furious and decided to walk home – (which is just through the common room and down the hallway). As she stomped down the hallway, her slippers kept falling off. Finally she stopped, took them off and launched them down the hallway. Even though Essa doesn't speak – she still uses her voice to communicate. She uses pitch and tone, and today she used them to communicate her extreme displeasure with Tony and Rob, both of whom also have Down syndrome. They hooted and hollered after her until Tina started to cry and it took Megan and me a full hour before everyone was settled down again.

I was kind of frustrated with Tony and Rob for provoking her. I know they did, because when they're together, they have a tendency to play a little rough, pretending to imitate the wrestling moves of their heroes from television, regardless of who they knock over in the process. Once they realized that Essa was really upset, they felt bad and wanted to apologize to her, but Essa had exhausted herself and I told them I would tell her how sorry they were. When I went in to peek in on her, she was already asleep. It's funny because there's this stereotype that all people who have Down syndrome are gentle and happy. I sure had a wry grin on my face as I watched those slippers sail through the air today. If only everyone could meet my Essa, then they'd know that she's not a "Down syndrome girl". She's a girl first, who happens to have Down syndrome – and who is just as apt to have an off day as the rest of us.

And amidst all these feelings and the lunacy of life – I can't escape the fact that it's crazy to think that I'll be working on what should have been my due date. It's impossible to predict what I might feel. Some days I seem to stumble blindly through, feeling nothing but the busyness of the season, other days I'm overcome with joy and gratitude and want to tell the world that I've been given a second chance... and then there are the dark days where I feel like I can't move for the sorrow and the fear and the loss – and it's all I can do to go through the motions of life, trying to drown out the drone of grief that rings in my ears.

Wednesday, December 19th, 2007

I worked with Megan again today. We found ourselves alone over coffee – something which rarely happens. There was a Christmas party happening at the community center and several volunteers had come with the Handi-Van and picked up all the residents. Because of regulations, one of us needed to be on call at the Manor and so both of us decided to stay and give the kitchen a good scrubbing. When we were done, Megan looked at me and asked me how I'm really doing.

She said it in that tone of voice that meant she really wanted to know. I was surprised by her sincerity, and the gentleness of her tone. I told her that I wasn't sure. I didn't think I could bear telling her yet that I'm pregnant when it still seems so new and fragile and still such a sacred thing – only shared between so few. I got up to pour myself another cup of tea to cover my shaking hands. If she noticed, she didn't say anything.

I heard a quick intake of breath, and in a gush of words that wasn't nearly as composed as the Megan I am used to, she stunned me by telling me that she had aborted her fourth baby over ten years ago. She quickly followed it with, "But it didn't really affect me, like your loss affected you."

She's a liar.

The tears brimmed over and made big splashes on the table and she picked up a cloth and pretended to intently examine the hem. I don't know what it was about today that made her open up to me. Maybe it was her way of telling me that she sees that I'm hurting. Maybe she was tired of keeping quiet – and keeping people comfortable – and she just needed to say it out loud. Whatever it was, once she started, she couldn't stop. She told me how Cam was never home at the time and they had already had three children in only four years. She said she felt like she never had any other options. Her mom had told her she was reckless and irresponsible for getting pregnant again in the first place. Her dad had offered to drive her to the clinic for the appointment since Cam was out of town. Her other three children were still so little and she was uninformed, unprepared and overwhelmed. Cam had told her that the other three were already more than he wanted. In a hurried phone conversation, he angrily told her to make the appointment. Three was too many, but four was beyond what a man could bear.

She said she still wonders about what would have happened if just one person would have told her to wait, to consider and to weigh the consequences. Then she stood up and wiped off the table, absently brushing the crumbs on the floor and said she was sorry, she didn't mean to barge in on me with her history and that of course it was a different thing than a miscarriage – she felt like she had ultimately made the choice, regardless of the pressure disguised as support from Cam, her parents and her doctor.

I had never met this Megan before.

I think I always pictured women who aborted their babies as these tougher than nails feminists – but in that moment of vulnerability, I realized that Megan is neither of those things. She seems cowed, and battered by her own guilt. She seems regretful – and sorrowful. When she let down the veil of brusque competence – there was a woman who made a choice thinking she didn't have one. I can't imagine adding the burden of remorse that she carries to the loss that already keeps me awake at night.

In my shocked silence, I'm ashamed to admit that I let the moment pass – and moments later we heard the van returning and the happy bubbling voices coming through the front door.

I wish I could have told her that I'm sorry for her loss. I wish I would have told her that I know Someone she can talk to about regrets that won't go away. I wish I wouldn't have let the moment pass and stupidly said nothing, when I had a chance to make a difference.

But I'll never forget that she let me in to her secret shame. I don't think I'll ever think of Megan as the mother of three again.

December 25th, 2007

I'm heading to work in five minutes. I can't button my pants. Not because they don't fit, but because any pressure feels painful. Brushing my teeth has become my most hated chore causing dry heaves at each and every attempt. When I looked at my face in the mirror today, I hardly recognized the exhausted girl that looked back at me. I have dark circles under my eyes and the crease from my pillow seam was snaking its way across my cheek. My hair is brittle and disobedient and my skin is pale with more blemishes than I can cover up.

Where's my pregnancy glow?

I told Jack I feel ugly and he said he couldn't hear me over the sound of my boobs expanding. Nice.

We decided to take a little holiday in the New Year as our Christmas gift to each other since it is such a funny year this year. We're planning on going to visit my mom and dad. I'm hoping that my sister Julie and her husband Dane can come meet us there. Jack's grandma still lives four blocks from my parents in the same little house Jack lived in with them when he first came to Canada. His grandpa died last year, and we know Grandma's lonesome and will welcome us with open arms after all the other family has gone home since our Christmas visit is so late.

Today, for our Christmas celebration, we made breakfast and had it in bed since neither one of us had to be at work until nine.

Best Christmas ever.

I bought Essa a little caddy for all her nail polish. We'll probably be alone tonight because all the other residents are going home to visit their families, but Essa's home is the Manor. Megan organized a full turkey dinner before everyone went home – so tonight we're ordering pizza and watching My Girl – Essa's favorite movie. I cry every single time we watch it so, like I said, Best Christmas Ever.

I wish Jack could come. Essa would love that. She loves Jack – and honestly, I think he's kind of sweet on her too.

January 1st, 2008

Happy Due Date, baby Tuesday.

Jack phoned from work and all he said was, "I know what day it is today."

I could hear people talking in the background and I knew that our conversation would be brief.

It was all I needed. Just the acknowledgement – the camaraderie that came from remembering for one tiny moment, our baby, made it feel like the two of us were ensconced in a secret hideaway. I could hear his breath on the line and feel the pounding of my heart in my ears as I said, "I do too."

Then he had to go, and I had to accept with regret that though this loss feels like it's mine alone, it's not. I wish that I could carry the burden of grief by myself, just so I could spare Jack the despair of it all – but it's not my sorrow to measure out, and Jack cannot be spared. There is comfort, though, in knowing that we are each walking this road – as individuals – in unison as every groan and sigh marks our passage along the road to healing.

I don't think I ever told you that I saw Tuesday's little body when she was born. Tuesday looked just like all the pictures in those pregnancy books I bought. I had wondered what to expect and I asked my doctor if my baby would be 'whole'. The doctor looked confused when I said that – and I don't know why that was the word I chose to use. Of course our baby was whole – tiny; but whole. Each individual finger – fearfully and wonderfully made.

And now – another one grows in the secret place where this first one died.

I'm beginning to wonder where my imaginings about heaven ends – and God's reality begins. The reality of death has forced me to take a closer look at what I believe about heaven, and I'm realizing that some of what has made up the image of heaven I carry about in my mind can't really be right after all.

I have always imagined it being the runner up prize when we've prayed for healing.

Somber angels with white robes and glowing halos - harps and streets of gold - Hawaii's climate - lounge chairs at the beach. Singing in a choir - getting all our questions answered.

No sadness - no grief - every tear wiped from every eye.

I've read my Bible. And I have cultural influences that have shaped the way that I think about this place. I have my own ideas of what seems right and fair to add to the mix.

And yet to me - to really get a grasp on Heaven seems to be impossible.

I find when I think about heaven; it's not this big comforting idea. There are too many unknowns. Is my baby a baby? What does it look like there? What work will I do? Is my child waiting for me there - or does time stand still and we'll get there at the same time? What do I know about heaven that isn't somebody's imaginings?

When I think about heaven - it makes me ache. It's too personal. It's too unimaginable. It's too foreign.

I need to understand a heaven that is able to mix with the reality of death. The tangible, heart-wrenching, 'how am I going to keep on keeping on' pain of death just won't mesh with a bed-time story book version of heaven. It's just not good enough when we're talking about my little Tuesday.

So, I was mulling this idea in my mind and all of a sudden, I stumbled on the comforting part.

God is there.

God is what I know about heaven. God loves me. He loves my children – both Tuesday, and this fresh burst of hope I'm carrying now. He has a purpose and a plan.

God is Good.

THAT is not somebody's imaginings - of white robes and angel wings with ethereal halos... that is TRUTH.

Heaven is only comforting because of God. Not as a half-fictional, half-reality based story to take away the tears for a just a moment – to play pretend for someone who has lost someone precious.

The God I serve has to be the personal God - who chooses to reach in and despite the fact that there is so much about life and death that is unimaginable - He makes me capable of Hope.

Heaven is faith-building.

So yeah, maybe there are days right now - when the thought of it feels foreign. But I know that because He's there - it's more home than here.

I remember when we went to Jack's aunt's funeral. She had been in a horrible car accident and was killed along with her two daughters. It was a horrifying ordeal and the whole family was devastated. His aunt was young and their two little girlies weren't even in school yet. The little chapel could have fairly burst at the seams with friends, family and the whole community gathering together to show support to Jack's uncle and to express their grief for such a crushing loss.

At the funeral, when his uncle got up to speak, there was a sudden hush. He described going to the scene of the accident right before the services; only days after their deaths. He said that even when he parked his car, and ran across the highway, he began to notice a feeling; an inkling that he was coming to a holy place. In the stillness of that overflowing chapel, he explained how he felt sure that this ground simply must be a holy place because it was the place where heaven opened up and welcomed his wife and two children. It was the place where God Himself welcomed the ones that he loved best into His kingdom. He described sitting in the grass with the dew fresh around him, the beginnings of morning traffic and the breeze seeming to fall from above. He said that for just a moment, he could see clearly that what remained when the sirens wailed and the ambulances arrived on the day of the accident; and what they were burying in the ground that very day – was just temporary. And that in the blink of an eye – every scene we look upon could be the portal to heaven as God's people leave their broken bodies behind, and gain access to the wonders above.

It gave me a whole different perspective on heaven to think of it as close as that. Like a curtain that could be opened to allow entrance to the most privileged guests, and then with a whoosh of heavenly air – it shuts again until it is time to usher in the next broken pilgrim.

I wonder if this new baby can still feel the whoosh of heavenly air from the departure of the tiny wisp of life that Tuesday was. I wonder if that whisper of heaven chased away the shout of death that permeated to the secret place inside me when that curtain lifted, and the brokenness of her body was revealed.

Thursday, January 3rd, 2008

I don't want to write about today, but there's a part of me that feels like I should.

I'm 13 weeks along today. I have gained 4 pounds, my morning sickness is starting so subside, and I had begun to believe that maybe we could pass this milestone of pregnancy without any problems at all.

I was drying off after my bath today when I noticed a smudge of blood. It took a minute for it to even sink in – that I was bleeding. I screamed for Jack, cursing myself for not being more careful with the water temperature. He burst in the room in his work clothes and I felt sick as I stood naked and trembling in front of him. My wet hair was lying stringy around my shoulders and I had mascara lines down my cheeks. I felt myself just slump to the floor. I couldn't even cover myself in my wretchedness. Jack's calm infuriated me and I wanted to scream at him to leave, but I needed him. I needed a voice of reason as I felt mine flitting away like a brown leaf in fall, finding itself caught in winter's first storm.

He told me, rather brusquely to get dressed. I did what he said and put in a pad and curled up on the edge of our bed. I just wasn't expecting it, and it almost seemed too much to bear at the exact stage of pregnancy we lost Tuesday.

I phoned the midwife who told me to come in and she would check me to see if there was anything to be concerned about. She said bleeding in pregnancy is a fairly common occurrence and she saw no need to panic now. She asked me how much I was bleeding and when I went to check, I found that the pad I put in was still clean. She said that I should come in for a check just to make sure, but that she wasn't worried.

We decided Jack should go to work. We have been planning our get away and he has been trying to get in as many hours as he can at the mill before we go. He felt like he just couldn't miss one more shift, so I told him (rather bitterly) to just go.

When I got to the midwife's office, she had laid out a clean sheet on one of the beds. She gave me a hug as I burst into tears the minute I stumbled through her door. It took what felt like forever for me to even calm down enough to speak with her. She said she was going to try to hear the baby's heartbeat with a Doppler, and even if she was unable to find one, that didn't mean we had cause to panic yet. She palpated my stomach first and smiled at me and told me she could feel the top of my uterus! I had no idea what she was trying to feel – and had felt nothing but a soft belly starting to bulge out of the top of my favorite jeans when I tried to feel anything at home. She got me to feel my own stomach, pressing way down low, and sure enough, there was a hard little mass just above my pubic bone. She winked at me and said, "That's a good sign."

Then she pulled out the Doppler and squirted a little bit of jelly on my stomach. The minute she put the wand to my belly, I heard this crackling, "Whoosh, Whoosh, Whoosh…" My midwife laughed. She actually laughed and said, "That was easy! There's your baby's heartbeat!"

I'm crying as I write this. It was the most beautiful sound in the world. Maybe I'm partial, or crazy, or emotionally exhausted, but I'm sure that what I heard was a very determined heartbeat. A heartbeat that with every measure stated, "Alive, alive, alive, alive…"

She said she still wanted to give me a check to make sure that all was well. When she checked me, she said, that my cervix was hard and closed and those were both good things. She said there were a lot of reasons for a little bit of blood in pregnancy and that I did the right thing coming in to get checked, but that she saw no reason to worry anymore about it.

And so – yet again – the burden that I pilfered from the One, who so ably carries it for me, is returned once more to rest where it belongs, at His feet.

Will this horrifying anxiety never cease to assail me? Is this motherhood? The constant nagging worry, the exercising of faith each time I step foot in the tub? Is this motherhood? The ecstasy of new life tempered with anxiousness to protect and the helplessness that comes when we realize that we're not able?

When I got home from the midwife's, the house was silent and empty. My laundry was all done and the house was already spotless and ready for our trip. I pulled off my jacket and sat at the kitchen table in the dim afternoon glow for a full ten minutes. I don't know what thoughts were rattling around in my mind, but suddenly, I was desperate to tell Essa I was pregnant. I needed – in the midst of my anxiety – to take a leap of faith and believe that I was going to have a baby. I jumped up from the table and fairly ran to my little car. It was still warm from my trip to the midwife, and it roared to life, as if it too wanted to share the joy of knowing that our baby lived. In a moment, I felt changed, and it felt natural to want to shout from the mountain tops the joyous news... like we had done the time before. When I got to the Manor, I went straight to the workshop where Essa was busily cutting strips of fabric. I asked her if she could come for coffee with me and while she skipped off to get her jacket, I told Sophie that I'd have her back in an hour.

We got out to the car and Essa was already fiddling with the radio before I even got in. As we pulled away from the Manor, I blurted the news that Jack and I were going to have a baby. I mistook her silence for not understanding, and I tried again, using different words, trying to be clear and make her understand. Then as I glanced sideways, I realized that she hadn't missed a word, she was just overcome on hearing my news. She grabbed my arm with mittened hands and with shining eyes vocalized her pleasure and hope.

Then I told her in mock severity not to tell anyone, and she threw back her head and laughed, waving her mittens in sheer joy.

Today was Jack's last day at work. Tomorrow, we're leaving to go see my mom and dad for our belated Christmas. I'm really excited to see them and to have everyone know that we're expecting again. I'm officially finished my first trimester, and tomorrow, I'll have carried this baby longer than I carried Tuesday. I feel anxious to cross that line. In a way, I feel a crazy sort of connection to this baby. Right at this stage, in these days I happen to know almost exactly what this baby most assuredly looks like. It is odd to have had that glimpse into the womb – it changed me to see life in its fragile beginnings – so worthy of awe, and deserving of grief. I'm certainly a different mother than I would have been, had I not lost Tuesday – and yet – when Tuesday died, the mother in me who had never lost a baby died too... so this baby is stuck with this grave young mother who is still reeling, and fiercely grateful – and there's a part of me that wonders if that will be good enough.

We had prepared an email to send to our closest circle of friends today, just to begin to let the news out because I have been so afraid to let anyone know– but I chickened out after our scare this morning. I'll send it tomorrow before we go. I included Mr. Henry as a recipient.

Oh, baby...

As the days have spread into weeks – I kept my secret...
Bringing out my knowledge of you
to admire in the dark before sleep came.
I watched my body begin to change - to accommodate you,
Little one,
into whom life was breathed by God Himself.
Your days were already numbered by the Creator of the
Universe and I praised Him
as I rested in the knowledge of His Goodness.

But now, the secret is leaked...
In whispers - hushed and sacred –
news of your impending arrival is beginning to spread.
Our circle of love – once only God and you
- next me - next papa –
is spreading further and further
as those who will love you for life hear the joyful news
that you're coming.
Jack's baby - hoped for, loved and expected
07-10-08

PART II

Friday, January 4th, 2008

There's something about getting in the truck and just going. It's a ten hour drive and we only have the long weekend, so we're planning on making the most of it. We got up at the crack of dawn. Jack started the truck up while I got the last of our things packed and ready to go, and within a half hour we were on the road. I thought I was going to freeze, walking the twenty or so steps from our back door to the running truck. I felt the cold freeze my eyelashes and prick my nose. I stepped carefully in the path Jack had shoveled in the fresh snow that had fallen in the night and pulled my jacket over my bare hand to open the icy handle. When I opened the door and climbed in, the heater was blasting and the radio was murmuring a welcome in the background. The dim overhead light beckoned as I climbed into our trusty steed, and blinked out when I closed the door. Suddenly, in the warmth and the dull glow of the running lights, with my seat rumbling like a beast, anxiously growling to begin, I felt like I was awaying on a secret adventure. I was tucked in, safe from the elements, and the snow swirling in angry ringlets outside. I was travelling with the one I love, and best of all, I was carrying our precious secret. In a minute, Jack came bounding from our house in his long, loping stride and I knew that our house was locked up tight, already waiting for our return, and we were off.

We stopped for hot chocolates an hour out of town, and it was still as dark as pitch. We don't always talk when we drive. Sometimes, like now, I'll write in my journal – or Jack will listen to the radio. Every once in awhile, he'll just start talking - about work, money, his family, our house. I have learned that when he does, I need to stop what I'm doing and pay very close attention. It doesn't seem like it's anything important when he tells me about the difficulty they've been having installing the new dryer at the mill – or that he wonders if the overtime he has been putting in will be enough to make an extra mortgage payment this year – but it is. It's like his first bumbling letters to me, at first they seemed careless and inconsequential... but over time, I noticed that scattered in those conversations about nothing – were the conversations that changed everything. Being married to Jack is like being on a lifelong treasure hunt – I never know what I will find when he first starts talking but I'm confident that if I listen long enough – I won't be disappointed.

If you were listening to us, you might think that our conversations sound a little one sided, because I always need so many more words to communicate my ideas than Jack does. One time, I remember trying to only speak as much as Jack did on a trip. If he would say a sentence to me, I would say one back. I spent a whole hour biting my tongue, when finally he turned to me and asked what was wrong, why was I being so quiet? I told him that I thought maybe since he was so quiet, he'd want me to be quiet too- I told him that maybe I should let him talk more, and I should listen. That's when he told me for the first time that he liked my noise. It has been an ongoing joke between us ever since.

I think that part of what Jack has always done so consistently for me is with very few words, he points my train of thought in a better direction. If my words, thoughts and actions begin to stray towards bitterness, he says something so casually - and without even a hint of judgment - and deflects my thinking and causes me to meander on in my verbiage towards forgiveness or understanding. If I start a blathering a judgmental rampage, he'll say something like, "Yeah, but man, have I ever been guilty of the same thing..." and without another word or a condescending cock of an eyebrow, he'll have broadened my perspective and allowed me to see another angle to a problem that I had been completely blind to before.

I have made it my goal to be more like Jack – to be a sounding board – the voice that dares him to choose better – the one who encourages his goodness and sifts the negative, letting the chaff float away unchecked and unmeasured.

Later –

We're still driving. Jack and I are having an unspoken battle. Every time he stops for gas or stops paying attention, I change the radio station. The minute he notices, he puts it back to the country station. We have been listening to soft rock for 10 minutes. I give him one more round of Whitney Houston before he notices...

We're getting closer. We stopped for lunch three hours ago and Jack figures we'll be there in another 45 minutes. We made fairly good time – the roads could have been better, but they could have been worse too. I phoned mom and dad an hour ago to let them know where we are and they said that Julie and Dane are already there and that we'll all have supper together tonight at their house. Dane owns his own furnace installation business, so he was able to take a few days off, and Julie just had to rearrange some shifts at the hospital so they could come meet us at Mom and Dad's. It's only a two hour drive for them, so they have been waiting since before lunch and are getting antsy for us to get there. I can't wait.

Oh! Darn it! Back to Alan Jackson! Well played, Jack... well played.

Still later –

Three entries in one day is what happens to me when we go on the road. We're here. Julie got our email about the baby this morning, so she was beside herself when we pulled into the driveway wanting to get all the details about her newest niece or nephew. Julie and I have always been incredibly close. These past five years, though, things have slowly begun to change as we've realized that we can't assume that the other still fits the mold that we knew so well in childhood. We've grown beyond those familiar grooves and crevices. We've been changed and influenced by our passions, our experiences – and the men we have married. The thing that doesn't change though is our love for each other. I know that no matter what happens, where I'm at or who's against me, my big sister's got my back.

When we were in elementary school, I was already bigger than Julie, even though she was two grades ahead of me. I was only in grade two, so she must have been in grade four. I was a bit of a loner – and one day at recess, I found myself being taunted by a "sixer" – our schoolyard term for the intimidating sixth graders that ruled the playground. The bully mocked me from behind; following me as I blindly stumbled away from the merry-go-round and around the swing set. As she followed me, her angry words confused me in my childish innocence until out of the corner of my eye; I saw a tiny flash of light as Julie came bounding apart from her circle of friends.

She was the littlest fourth grader in the school, but she was feisty. "Hey KID!" she shouted, "Why don'cha pick on someone your own size?"

At that moment, the bell mercifully rang and we thought we were safe. Julie wrapped her arm protectively around my shoulder and started walking me towards the school. All of a sudden the bully hit Julie from behind and they both hit the ground in a cloud of dust.

Julie and I still laugh about the day she took my beating for me. But that's what kind of a big sister she has always been. That's why I'm always surprised when we disagree about things now.

Julie was already two years into her nurses training when I graduated high school. I think she assumed that I would follow in her footsteps. Actually, I kind of thought I would follow in her footsteps too – we have always had such similar bents. When I opted for less training and following Jack across the country, I think she was disappointed in some way.

And then, there's the baby thing too. While Jack and I have been wanting a baby since we got married – she says that she and Dane have been on birth control since they got married; two years longer than Jack and I –and have no plans to get off it in the near future... and if I'm honest – that makes me feel disappointed in some way. I'm not sure what it is about her cavalier attitude towards motherhood that makes me feel frustrated, but it does.

Tonight at supper, in the midst of the talk about our baby, Julie started asking me all kinds of medical questions. At first it was alright and I didn't mind my nurse sister asking me how I was feeling and if my morning sickness was getting any better. But then she wanted to know if our midwife had ordered a Nuchal Translucency test. I told her our midwife hadn't even mentioned it, trying to cover the fact that I had never heard of such a thing. She said maybe we should look for another midwife because it should have been offered as a matter of course.

I asked her what it was for, and she said it was offered in the first trimester as a screening test for chromosomal disorders. And then she said the most bizarre thing. "Granted, it's usually for termination purposes, but regardless, if there was something that wrong with your baby, wouldn't you want to know?"

Jack answered her, "I don't know. I guess it would depend on how the earlier diagnosis would help the baby. If it's mainly for termination purposes, it's not something we want anything to do with."

Then she asked us if we were planning on refusing the triple screen test too. I felt all flustered because I had no idea what that was either – or that I should be getting all this testing done. I felt like her insinuation was that any good mother would have all these little boxes checked off better than I did.

Jack saved me by telling her we were going to the midwife on the fourteenth and we'd ask about any tests we needed to take. She just told him we'd better hurry because I was already finished my first trimester and I would need to take some of these tests by my 15th week.

Mom and dad didn't say very much during the whole exchange – and honestly, this was such a small part of the night, but it's the part that's keeping me from falling asleep right now at midnight as Jack snores beside me.

When we were getting ready for bed, I talked for about twenty minutes straight about my frustration with Julie, my confusion over the necessity of testing and my feeling of inadequacy for not even knowing what Julie was talking about.

While I talked, Jack brushed his teeth, changed his clothes and climbed into bed. When I finished, he yawned, rolled over and mumbled, "Tests are dumb anyway." And he went to sleep.

Now I'm sitting here, writhing, while he has been sleeping for an hour already. I just might poke him.

Saturday, January 5th, 2008

I'm hiding in the basement. Jack and Dane are watching sports with my dad and Julie and mom are looking through some old pictures that mom's trying to sort. In a bit, we're going to see Jack's grandma, but first I needed a rest.

Julie and I went shopping today. She bought me three maternity tops and the sweetest clips for my hair. She loved the sky blue porcelain teapot we got her. I almost didn't want to give it to her; I had so fallen in love with it myself. It had kind of regal gold plating on the handle and the spout and around the lid – but was still so plucky and fresh looking in its cheeky blue. I'll have to pick up the orange cream and sugar that complement it for her birthday.

She told me she's really excited about the baby – and I knew she meant it as an apology for last night.

We haven't seen each other since before I lost Tuesday. Most of my friends dropped off the face of the earth in those first weeks after it happened. I didn't know how I was supposed to grieve so I ended up not answering the phone or emails, or even the doorbell when it rang.

Julie wouldn't let me ignore her.

She phoned Jack on his cell and asked to speak to me, she sent me flowers right away and then in the next week, she sent me a package with teas, lip balm and a thick copy of At the Back of the North Wind. She emailed me until I couldn't ignore her anymore and then she listened while I cried on the phone, and said nothing when words would have been pointless or offensive.

I feel bad for writing about being frustrated with her when she has been one of the few that has known instinctively how to be compassionate to me.

Today after we finished shopping, we met up with mom and had a girl's lunch out. Dad and the boys stayed home and had leftovers. Mom took us to a quiet bistro that sells the best grilled cheese sandwiches I have ever had. They have every kind of bread or cheese you can imagine – Julie and mom had grilled brie and goat cheese with green tomatoes on whole wheat bread, but I'm still too paranoid from everything I have read on my 'don't do' list, so no soft cheeses for me! I stuck with a pepper Jack cheese (in honor of my Jack) on focaccia.

PS I just read Jack the part about my sandwich and he says he wants me to write that his leftovers were good too. He named them Anna. Jealous much?

Sunday, January 6th, 2008

So much has happened in the last day and I want to record every bit of the jumbled emotions I'm feeling at the moment.

Last night, Jack and I slipped away to go and visit his grandma. We had planned on visiting with her at her house for a couple of hours and then mom had invited us to bring her back to their place for supper.

When we got there, we knew right away that something wasn't right. His usually tidy, efficient little grandma came to the door, looking tired and confused. When we went inside, our alarm grew as we realized that her speech seemed slurred and that there was most definitely something that was not quite right. We asked her how she was, and she had difficulty responding. Jack sat with her while I phoned Julie. Julie told me to call 9-1-1 and that she would be right over. She said it sounded like she could have had a stroke, and it would be wise not to waste any time.

Jack rode in the ambulance with his grandma and we phoned Jack's uncle and aunts to tell them what was going on. They were all genuinely shocked and said that she had been the picture of health when they had all gathered for Christmas. Jack's aunt who lives the closest said that she would be here tonight and we promised to keep the other two updated. Jack phoned his parents too, but nobody was home. He left a message on their machine, and I imagine they'll call when they get it.

By the time Jack's aunt got here, the doctors had already confirmed Julie's suspicions. She has had a stroke. They're keeping her in the hospital for now while they try to figure out how bad it is and what they need to do for her. Julie brought me home last night while Jack stayed at the hospital until they sent him home. Now, Jack has been gone all day, staying at the hospital with his aunt, and then going to pick up some things his aunt thought his grandma would want from the house. I'm hoping he'll be home soon now.

I feel so bad for her. Jack said the doctor suggested that he didn't think it had been very long that she was in confusion before we got there, and if that's the case, he has high hopes for the early treatment that they have begun, but there's no way to know for sure just yet. I guess time will tell.

There was something about tonight that is sketched in watercolor across the back of my mind. I don't want it to ever fade, because the picture of it so moves me and it reminds me why I fell in love with Jack in the first place.

When Grandma answered the door, fumbling for the doorknob for what seemed an eternity, and then slowly opening it and leaning on it for strength, I think I was frozen at first - stunned to see her standing looking so disheveled and incoherent and exposed, so unlike the Grandma we have always known. Jack didn't need time to let that information sink in. He wrapped his arms around her and said, "Oh, Grandma – I'm so glad we came."

Gently, he took her hand, and led her into the house – whispering into her ear and gesturing for me to phone Julie. At each step – he calmly explained to his grandma what was happening, and why we were calling for help. She clung to him with her left hand and he wouldn't leave her side – even for a minute. I almost felt like an intruder – with my bumbling efforts to help.

Jack normally isn't soft or compassionate – but today, when he saw his grandma, so needy and insecure, he held her so delicately and tenderly that he gave back to her – even in her confusion – the dignity that sickness had taken away.

As we waited for the ambulance to arrive to take her to the hospital, suddenly I remembered how Jack's mother had prayed for me – and I told Jack I wanted to pray for Grandma too. I took her hands as tenderly as I could – and kissed them. Then I gathered my courage, and with words that were bolder than my spirit felt – I began to ask the One I love to watch over Grandma. My Father – who comforted me in my loss, Jehovah Rapha – God, our healer met with me as I reached out to Him in desperation. As I spoke, I found I didn't feel like a stranger in His presence. Simple words tumbled from my mouth as we heard the wail of the ambulance arriving. I stepped back and Grandma reached for me. She was trying to tell me something. The EMT's started talking to Jack and it felt like the peace of the preceding moment had been shattered by utter chaos. I strained my ears to hear and tried to catch what she was saying as her eyes locked on mine – I'm almost positive I caught the words, 'thank you'.

Monday, January 7th, 2008

We're on the road again. I decided to wait until we were in the truck to write again. There is so much to write – if I want to record the bewilderment of these days.

This morning, Julie helped me get the house back in order after our invasion on Mom's basement. As we stripped sheets and gathered damp towels, out of the blue, she started talking about my work at the Manor.

She asked me if working at the Manor made me afraid to have a baby. She wanted to know if working with people who have special needs made me paranoid that our little one would have special needs. She said that she couldn't do what I do – and that she knew that she couldn't ever cope if she ever had a baby that wasn't normal.

I didn't even know where to begin, so I was silent for a minute, thinking about how I should answer. But the more I was silent, the more she expanded and the angrier I felt. Her words seemed abrasive and struck at my emotional, sensitive heart.

What is normal anyway? Where do we draw the line that measures an acceptable level of humanity? Does Essa not make the cut because of her 'designer genes'? Does Tina not measure up because of her cerebral palsy? What about the precarious position that Jack's grandma finds herself in? Is it possible to lose our distinction of adequacy through illness or circumstance?

What about people who are cruel or arrogant? What about abusers like Essa's foster family? Are these not illnesses of the soul? Why do we get so worked up about the existence, and the special care required for the vulnerable whose bodies are weak– and then end up ignoring the sicknesses that eat away at what matters most, what makes us human, sicknesses that will ultimately leave us rancid and depraved?

Megan and I have sometimes talked about the parents of the residents – the stability of Nikki's family versus the utter abandonment that Essa went through. Would Jack and I be able to pull off what seems so effortless to Nikki's jovial family if our little one needed us to? I imagined all the physiotherapy appointments that they make, the surgeries that Essa went through when she was a premature newborn, clinging to life. I imagined the doctor appointments, the occupational therapy and Essa's frequent hospitalizations. I imagined the sorrow at knowing that my child's life would be vastly different from most people... the constant staring and hurtful comments from people who have never learned how much it stings. As I touched my swollen abdomen, I imagined all the things our baby would miss out on, if they missed out on our culture's definition of, "normal".

But then another image flashed through my mind. I remembered the way Nikki's dad swings her in the air as she squeals and clings to his neck. I remembered the way Essa threw back her head and laughed her gurgling laugh; clapping her sweet, short hands together when I grabbed her hairbrush and did my impromptu version of Doo Wah Diddy. I remembered the way she blushed furiously the first time she met Jack and he brought her a bouquet of daisies.

I pictured the way her almond eyes brim with tears and sparkle like diamonds when she's frustrated. I pictured the way she holds out her fingers so bewitchingly when she wants me to paint them, and the way her tongue rests on her bottom lip when we're watching My Girl. I remembered the way she stole Nikki's earrings and brought them to us a hundred times before we finally gave in and took her to get her tiny little ears pierced with dainty golden studs.

And, I pictured the way her slippers sailed through the air as she stomped furiously down the hallway to her room.

When I spoke, I wasn't angry anymore.

I told Julie how I had been going through Essa's file one day, adding the records from her most recent hospital stay. As I put the papers in order, I happened upon a document that was filled out with her full name, Essence Crowther. Seeing her name written out like that struck me, and kept nagging at my conscience. I contemplated it for days before I decided to just look it up in my dictionary.

I found that Essence means heart, or significance, and is synonymous with life.

How appropriate that her name so exquisitely defines what we find impossible to measure.

I tried for days to track down who had given Essa her name in the first place, and I got nowhere. I imagined that somewhere, a nurse, or a foster family had offered an inspired suggestion - a name so poignant that just the utterance of it would give pause to those who met her. Essa reminds me on a daily basis the heart of what makes us human. Her challenges don't make her less human – but our inability to see the value in her life? Well, the way I see it, that does take away from our humanity. I told Julie that I wish everyone could have the experience of working where I work. The Manor, and each of its unique residents - have all been an indescribable gift to me. My work there has given me valuable resources that could help us if we ever did have a child with special needs – but more importantly, working there has reminded me to look to my Father to define the essence of humanity – not a broken, merciless culture.

Julie seemed kind of taken aback with my honesty, and she said that I was probably right, but that in her line of work, she saw the worst case scenarios and that sometimes she was forced to wonder if we wouldn't be better off without all the pain and heartache that a lot of these medical conditions bring with them. She mentioned a baby that was carried to term, despite the doctor's warnings that the child's diagnosis was incompatible with life. We sat down on the made bed as she described the agony as the family gathered to meet the wee one they had been aching for. She said the tiny boy lived only hours – and she couldn't bear to watch the young mother groaning in sorrow as they said goodbye. She begged off the remaining minutes of her shift and went home shaking, wondering why they had followed through on a pregnancy they knew would end in heartbreak.

It left me wondering what the point of life is. Is it supposed to be lived without agony? How is God's glory revealed when we snuff out life as soon as we detect the potential for discomfort? What are we saying of life when we pressure parents to extinguish the lives of the little ones they should be willing to die to protect? I thought of Megan – and the pressure that she felt to abort her tiny baby, seemingly because its life appeared to be superfluous. We have been indoctrinated to believe that abortion is a woman's right – a woman's choice, and yet it seems like there is another agenda at work. And the work of this sinister agent bends a woman to its pressures to ease the comfort of the herd. It weeds out the weak. Our tiniest and most vulnerable are in danger as well as the dying and the aged. Is this what we've become, a society that sees life as disposable? Are we too pristine to be in the presence of heartache – too busy getting rid of the imperfect to see that our comfort was bought at a price?

Jack's tapping my journal. I think he wants to visit. I'm glad to be going home and to sleep in my own bed. My mind is twisting in the turmoil of thoughts that weren't as urgent before. It seems that in becoming a mother, I have been forced to put to rest the mundane discussion of the hypothetical and in its place, I find a ferocious, protective, primal reaction to culture's reality. I'm exhausted, and in my exhaustion, I feel a keen sense of tenderness for the little one who grows inside. I feel relieved that we haven't tested our child and opened ourselves to the scrutiny of a callous field that would try to measure the value of this little one, who is already so desperately loved. The best part of going away is coming home, and the peace of home pulls me toward it like a mother's embrace.

Tuesday, January 8th, 2008

We got home in the wee hours. Our house was dark and chilly but we turned up the heat and by the time we were finished unpacking the truck, it was toasty warm. Jack has to work today, but I don't have to go back until tomorrow, so I'm staying home and baking cookies.

I wonder what it will be like to be home all the time with a little baby. While Jack still goes out and interfaces with the world – what will it be like to spend my days interfacing with my own tiny child? Right now, it's a treat to get to stay home and bake – because it happens so rarely. Will the novelty wear off?

I hear women say that it can be boring, monotonous or lacking in mental stimulation to be a stay at home mom. I'm beginning to wonder what kind of a mom I will be.

I sent Megan our announcement email before we left, and I'm sure she'll ask me soon what my plans are for work. I hope I'm ready to answer her when she does.

Monday, January 14th, 2008

Our writing class met for the first time since the holidays today. Every single one of us has decided to continue. It was kind of neat because Kevin brought something to read to us, which was a first.

Kevin has always seemed so miserable – like he's ravenously hungry, but not for food. His hair hangs down, covering most of his acne scarred face. He rarely speaks, and when he does, his words are always edged with contempt. He wears his jeans hanging almost to his knees with a black hoodie pulled up, covering his earphones. He comes with Ryan, but I don't know how close the two of them are. When Kevin introduced himself at the beginning of the year, he told us that he hoped he could learn to write, or his English teacher had promised to fail him. Ryan piped up with a goofy smile, "Me too!" and we all laughed.

Mr. Henry said he would do everything in his power to help them graduate, and he has. I have noticed him helping Kevin before and after we meet with his homework from his regular classes. He has made subtle efforts to find in his work the words that are salvageable, the sentiments that are worthy and the pieces that are praiseworthy.

I remember the first time Mr. Henry admired a paragraph Kevin had written– I watched Kevin's dark eyes that wouldn't leave Mr. Henry's face, carefully measuring his words, listening for sarcasm, waiting for the disparaging litany of failures to follow – but it never did. I have noticed Mr. Henry deliberately, gently, cautiously reaching a hand of friendship to Kevin. He masterfully creates situations that allow Kevin to succeed – and like a hungry, wounded dog – Kevin is slowly beginning to respond to the consistent kindness that Mr. Henry extends.

Today, he shyly held up his hand and told Mr. Henry that he had worked on the special assignment he had been given over the holidays, and he was ready to read it to us. Mr. Henry didn't show his surprise, he just told him to go ahead and explain what he was going to read. He told us that his high school English Literature class had studied the story of Oedipus Rex. I barely remembered it from my high school days.

He quickly summarized the part of the story he had focused on.

He said his favorite part had come in the middle, where the seemingly unbeatable Sphinx held a city hostage with an unsolvable riddle: What walks on four legs in the morning, two legs at noon, and three legs at night – with the solution obviously being that a man crawls on four legs in infancy, two legs in adulthood and uses a cane as a third leg in old age.

Mr. Henry had asked Kevin to re-tell just that small part of the famous tale, in modern day colloquialisms. It was hilarious. I wish I had the whole thing, but I remember parts like, "That Sphinx was a hot mess, yo. She was torqued that he had Mcgyvered her riddle, so she offed herself from them city walls. Oedipus was all, 'BOOM shakalaka'"

We howled and cheered when he finished, and Mr. Henry said he completed the assignment beautifully. He wanted us to see that as foreign as some of the Old English, or Shakespearian plays seemed to us, even in modern day English there are dialects and lingoes that can be just as difficult to decipher.

Kevin let his hair fall in his face and slouched farther than ever into his seat, crimson creeping up his neck under the attention, so Mr. Henry moved on.

He said he wanted us to think about the way the solution to this riddle depended on us expanding our perspective. He wanted us to see if we could choose something in life and broaden our views enough to see it three different ways, like the Sphinx did with the three stages of walking for man. I have an idea – but I'm not sure how to flesh it out yet. We'll see if I can get it down for our next class.

Tuesday, January 15ᵗʰ, 2008

Hurray!! Another midwife appointment today! It feels like each one I tick off brings me leaps and bounds closer to our baby. Even though I am only just shy of 15 weeks pregnant, I feel like I have been pregnant forever.

Jack was off today, so he decided to come with me. Once again, there wasn't anyone using the birthing center, so we decided to use the living room upstairs for our appointment. This time, I accepted the tea that Sam offered and I cleared my throat, wondering how to approach the topic of testing that Julie had considered so important. I decided first to ask her about the test that Julie said I should have already had.

My midwife looked a little surprised and told me that in general she and the midwives that she practiced with tried to avoid unnecessary ultra sounds. She said that they only offered the Nuchal Translucency test if a mom was of advanced maternal age, or if she requested to have it done. Even in those cases where there is an increased risk, she said, she personally isn't a big fan of excessive testing. She said that over the years, she had seen far too many false positives to be convinced of the reliability of the test. She felt responsible that often parents were unnecessarily confused or frightened, or that they made decisions about termination when the information didn't seem to be very accurate.

As she leaned back in her chair, sipping her steaming coffee, she told us a story about the birth of a baby with Down syndrome that she had attended last year. The mother had declined all tests, and had actually declined regular prenatal care, deciding to do her own record keeping, and using her own knowledge and skills to care for her pregnancy. It was her eighth pregnancy, and there were no complications. Sam said that she had no concerns at all about this mother taking on her own care, and that she knew if she would be needed, the mother would contact her.

The pregnancy progressed beautifully, and Sam said the mother stopped in from time to time just to have the occasional check up. Four days before her due date, the midwives were called in the night. The mother had gone into labor and was ready to have their support. When they arrived, the mother breathed between contractions, telling them in a perplexed tone, 'There's something different going on this time...'

The midwives had stayed with her, and watched her labor, encouraging her until finally; she delivered her baby in the pool of water she was kneeling in. When she brought the baby out of the water, she held her tiny son over her shoulder, relieved that it was over and that her squalling baby had arrived. As she caught her breath, and began to get comfortable, she pulled him back so she could take a look at him, and that's when they all saw that he had some of the characteristics that are consistent with Down syndrome. The midwives had paused, giving the mother and father room to admire their little boy – and as the father bent down and kissed the mother's wet head, she just breathed, "You..."

Sam said they waited and watched, holding their breath, feeling the thickness of the air in the room as the baby cried gustily and the father let his son's hand curl around his thumb. There was no doubt in those moments that all in the room were aware of the likelihood of a Down syndrome diagnosis. In the silence that followed, the mom finally finished her sentence, "You're the one we have been waiting for."

Sam smiled a soft remembering smile and said she hasn't been convinced about prenatal diagnosis ever since that night. "Sometimes it's good and works well, and the early diagnosis helps parents and medical staff to be better prepared for the unique needs that the baby may have, and that's alright. But sometimes," she laughed gently, "babies just need to make their own introductions..."

It made me start questioning all of the testing there was to be done. Apparently, they were supposed to recommend various tests for sexually transmitted diseases, a triple screen – whose main objective was diagnosing Down syndrome for termination purposes, and a glucose test for gestational diabetes. There were also blood tests, urine analysis and an extra ultrasound that were offered in addition to my midwife appointments.

All of a sudden, I felt like running. I felt like a little alien being poked, prodded and tested – and I didn't like it. As my midwife filled out requisitions and told me how to go about booking my appointments at the lab, I was barely able to choke out, "Do I have a choice?"

She laughed out loud. "Of course you have a choice! There are many of those tests that I would refuse myself if I were in your shoes. You're obviously a bright woman who is capable of making healthy, informed choices for you and your baby. Go home with the paperwork I've given you, do your research, phone me if you have any questions and do what your God-given instincts tell you to do!"

Jack looked at me, and right in front of a still chuckling Sam, he mouthed the words, "I like her."

I decided I did too.

Afterwards, I asked if we could hear the heartbeat again. I lay down on the couch, and we heard that precious whooshing sound and I felt the tears roll from my eyes back into my ears. Then, she felt my uterus that was becoming a hard little lump in my lower abdomen and measured it with a tape.

Baby? She said that you were perfect. She said your heartbeat was glorious, and that you were measuring just what you should be measuring.

While she took my blood pressure, she asked me if I had any other questions or concerns. I told her I thought we had covered quite enough ground for one day, so she said she'd see us again in a month.

When we left, I checked my watch. We had been in there for an hour and a half. I shoved a couple of books from their 'give and take' library into my purse. I was excited to get home and start reading. Jack took my hand so that I wouldn't slip on the ice and asked if I wanted to get pizza tonight.

He's getting it as I write, so I'd better quit and get the salad made before he gets home.

Thursday, January 17th, 2008

I feel like all week I count down to Thursdays. All week, I look forward to the day I can add another week onto my growing total of weeks. Today, I am 15 weeks pregnant. Doesn't that sound like a nice substantial number? I feel bloated, but Jack says he can't tell I'm pregnant. When we were back home for our holiday, I bought a pair of maternity pants. I tried them on to show Jack and he said I looked ridiculous. I guess the maternity clothes will have to wait a little longer then. I find myself sticking out my belly in the mirror, imagining that nice, full, round tummy belonging to me. Jack caught me the other day and he has been mocking me mercilessly ever since, sticking out his flat tummy every time I walk into the room.

But then last night, he laid his head on my belly and didn't try to be funny when he whispered to my bellybutton; 'Hi.' Before he rolled over and went to sleep. I feel like I could almost miss those moments of tenderness if I blinked in the wrong instant.

Work has been crazy lately. The Workshop sold out of most of their inventory at Christmas time, so we have been cleaning out the storage room and figuring out where to start re-stocking. Essa was so pleased that the quilts sold so well this year. We even had a couple of people come to the Workshop to see if they could get them custom made, so we may start doing more of that if there seems to be a demand for it.

When I got back to work after our holiday, I found a little wrapped package waiting for me on the kitchen table. I was working with Sophie and she said that Megan had left it for me at the end of her shift. When I unwrapped it, there was a tiny fleece quilt, just the right size for a baby – and a card from Megan that said in her swirling penmanship, "Truly pleased for you. Love, Megan"

It's our first baby gift. Essa looked all conspiratorial and pleased and I knew that she must have helped Megan pick it out, and that made me love it even more.

Saturday, January 19th, 2008

I have been working on my assignment for Mr. Henry. When we were first talking about it in class, I thought of the differences between my pregnancies – one that will only exist as a memory, and one that will presumably also become a memory – evidenced by our child's presence many years from now. After giving it a lot more thought, I decided that maybe the natural third perspective would be the perspective of one who had not been able to have a pregnancy at all. I almost have it ready to hand in.

Love Letters

To the child that cannot be –
You came, you lived, you grew.
Warm soft skin and apple breath,
Sweet small lump of life,
Gone too fast – gone too fast to
Shrieking laughter and childhood games.

To the child that cannot be –
You came, you lived, you left.
No pictures in your baby book.
Sweet small lump of life,
Gone too fast – gone to fast to
Memory.

To the child that cannot be –
You never came. You never came,
You never lived, you'll never be.
Oh, how I ache to hope for you.
Sweet small lump of life,
Gone too fast – gone too fast to
Moving on.

Sunday, January 20th, 2008

I went to church today.

Jack was working and I dreaded going on my own, but I did it anyway.

Somewhere between the hand shaking and the singing and the sermon, I began to bring out all the questions that have been loitering in the fringes of my mind about God.

I started to wonder if I trust Him enough to be laid bare – I wonder what I'm made of, and if it's good enough. I mean, despite my best efforts to be good and to imagine myself making the right choices in horrible circumstances, I don't know, I *can't* really know - until the defining moment that makes clear the kind of a person that I've have allowed myself to become.

I have heard stories of martyrs - the persecuted church, stories of love so overwhelming and humbling; people who made difficult - impossible - choices in the name of Love. And still, most of the time I sit, wondering about my own discomfort, and wishing for my own happiness.

And it struck me, as I sat in that familiar building - that I'm starting to feel like this life is my study hour, and I need to dig in to hear that still small voice – to prepare my heart for the journey ahead.

I have begun to pray when the anxiety begins to overcome me - that when God has me walk through the furnace, will He please give me what I lack so that the question isn't: What am I made of? But is instead: What can God make of me? Maybe I have gotten so wrapped up in my failings that I forgot that my failings don't negate God's truth. The truth of God's love and sacrifice doesn't depend on me getting all the answers right.

Who cares what I'm made of, when the One I love gives beauty for ashes? I want so badly to be in a place of complete surrender, where my will becomes His will, where my instincts are His.

What can You make me, God?

And so, this morning, I hope that the tiny shift in perspective brings me a little closer to Him. It's so hard to put aside so many of the things I have always thought about God and to replace them with new ideas, even when I know they must be true. For example, when I went to church today, I couldn't help analyzing so many of the worn out expressions that I heard as people commented on the news about our baby.

"Everything is sure to work out for you guys this time, I just know it..."

"God knows you deserve this happiness..."

"God knows what you can handle and He wouldn't let you get pregnant again if He isn't going to give you a baby this time."

I felt sort of exasperated. How do they know what my Father has planned for me? Could it be that God has something greater for us than our happiness? How many times have I heard those phrases, "As long as you're happy... As long as the baby's healthy..."Is that the greatest goal that we can have for our little ones? For ourselves? Are health and happiness as good as it gets? Could it be... that there is something more valuable out there?

What can You make me, God?

What could He do with those seasons of suffering, if I let him? What if He allows those refining moments; those

moments that seem devoid of happiness, to build into us –
holiness – so that we can be set apart for His use.

Why does it seem that when we aren't happy, we
question God's Goodness?

God doesn't lack Goodness because I'm *too near sighted
to see* that He's giving me something far more precious than
my own comfort. I know that He heard me when I cried. He
has compassion. He knew it might hurt to be stretched - and
brought to a place of surrender and yet... in His Goodness - He
still allowed it. I'm learning that what comes from His hand
might bring happiness or sorrow, comfort or aching discomfort,
but in this study hour, I want to let myself be found.

Monday, January 21st, 2008

Today Les told us that his daughter-in-law is expecting
their 47th grandchild. He laughed and said that it's about
time, since it will be their 47th wedding anniversary next
month. He seemed to want to tell us more so Mr. Henry asked
how he would incorporate this newest child into the story he is
creating. Les kind of sighed and said he has been having a
hard time with just that thing. This newest baby is the first
child of his youngest son who is only twenty-two. He said that
this son was born when he and his wife were already "knee
deep in their forties". They were busily raising their other nine
children and they hadn't had a baby in the house for four
years. He said a part of him just thought those baby years
were finished. One day, he got home from work and found
his wife crying at the kitchen sink. When he asked her what
was wrong, she started laughing with tears streaming down
her cheeks and cried, "Wrong? What could be wrong? Today,
there's only what's right." And then she told him about the
baby that would be coming in the next spring, to their mutual
delight and surprise.

"God knows they're all blessings, but it sure felt like a
special kind of miracle when we brought that little guy home."
Les continued with a wistful smile on his face. "And now, to
see him come to us, grinning and proud with his pretty little

wife on his arm to tell us he's making us grandparents again – I just don't even have the words for that kind of joy."

Mr. Henry paused for what seemed like a long time, and then he said he wanted us all to try something. He said that as Les was talking, it occurred to him that it would be a good exercise to think of what it is we want to pass on to future generations – to our children and grand-children – and to the world at large. He said he'd like us to write a letter, to a child not yet born – to proclaim a legacy to a generation that has not yet come.

Ryan said that the assignment wasn't fair, because by the time he has grandchildren, the world will have combusted in some giant nuclear explosion. Mr. Henry smiled and told him that his assignment would be toughest of all then; he would need to write a message of hope to that last generation.

Then Kevin said in a barely audible voice from the back of the room, "But what if there is no hope?"

Mr. Henry replied, "There is always hope."

Tuesday, January 22nd, 2008

Mr. Henry's assignment won't leave me alone.

I had a dream last night.

I have been dreaming constantly in recent months; mostly shadows and imaginings – nothing clear and tangible – until last night.

Last night was different.

I dreamed Jack and I were parents to a tiny army of children, just like Les and his wife. I dreamed that over the delectable years of our marriage, we added sons and daughters, each one bringing the joy that I saw on Les' face as he described the arrival of his tenth child. In my dream, it was night, and all was dark and quiet, and I held our youngest, a little boy – in a room with dim lights and a tiny cradle. His eyes fluttered and faltered, and I knew that just as he was perched precariously on the edge of sleep, so too was I perched precariously on a single grain in the sands of time, and that it was about to slip from beneath my feet, in the beautiful, merciless twist and tumble that time has about her. I knew that as his eyelashes fluttered – and his chest began to rhythmically rise and fall – that that precious bit of time would in another breath be over, and that grain of sand after it's hurtling fall through the hourglass would land; mixed and jumbled with the other moments of these precious years in the sands below. I tried desperately to drink in the tiny one – as his mouth pursed and sucked the air, his hand, once waving, now paused in midair as he began to drift. I memorized his features and breathed in his baby scent – the longing of my subconscious being sustained for a moment by the baby of my dreams.

When I woke, I got up, and with the image of the babe of my dreams fresh in my mind, I wrote my imagined tale of motherhood.

To the Great, Great Grandchildren...

To the great, great grandchildren of Ephraim Magnus; Maybe a hundred years from now - one of you will stumble upon this - and in your memory the name Ephraim Magnus will conjure up the image of an old man. I imagine his name will make you smile and tell the stories of how he loved his wife, bounced babes on his knee - and talked well of his mama.

That thought makes me smile; are my imaginings correct? But right now, that old man is my son - and I am his mama - and I delight in the rolls on his baby thighs and his baby crows and coos as his eyes flutter and fall and he drifts off into sleep.

I want to tell you something that may not have occurred to you. But it occurs to me as I muse on the significance of my little one - and the possibilities for his life... his family, his lineage, his influence...

You were a long shot

Descendants of my wee babe, he was a ninth pregnancy, a seventh child - a third son - for my husband and I. Our little Ephraim was a surprise. He was a tiny blessing in baby flesh - given to us by the grace of God - who sees the impact of this gift. Not just in our lives - in this generation - in this noisy household - to this grateful mama, but our Loving Father sees the impact that this generational line will have a decade from now - a century from now - a millennium from now - as the seven shoots that God blessed us with grow and flourish...and wither and die -and their offspring in their season and time come to blossom and bloom too.

I guess in short...I believe that God had you in mind when he blessed me with my little son.

Oh, children – my heritage - I have no doubt that He has a work in mind for you all to accomplish with what strength and talents he bestowed upon you. Listen to His voice.
I can't wait to learn of the impact of our little surprise - our much loved babe...your great, great grandfather,

Ephraim Magnus.

Oh, Father - it's as though for a moment - I can see much farther than my dim earth bound eyes should... light years ahead - through generations that will worship You and serve You. Take these little ones, Father - and bless the tiny buds that might never have been - that will be fruitful followers of the One I love.

Monday, January 28th, 2008

I have been reading and researching and talking to friends – and I just feel so lost. Sam gave me resources to check out, and she told me to feel free to make a doctor's appointment if I wanted to get a second opinion from someone who might have a different viewpoint. I phoned Julie and she gave me some websites to check out too.

Maybe it's my lazy nature, but part of me just wants to be told what to do. I want there to be one right way, one right choice, and I want to be shown what it is. Instead, the more that I research, the more confused I get and the more alternative viewpoints I discover.

Jack is as perplexed as I am. He says he trusts my judgment, but I don't want to be trusted.

We have decided a few things. After much deliberation, we decided to get the blood work and urine analysis done, but only as they pertain to a healthy pregnancy. We figured that's a pretty small inconvenience, and we can see the potential benefits to having those done. I'm refusing all the testing for sexually transmitted diseases on principle, and we also decided not to do the glucose test. After much reading and agonizing, it just seemed like one that we'd rather skip. Then there's the matter of the ultrasound. I think we've decided to go for it. I'm still on the fence about it, but I feel like for this one, I'm going to choose to look at the pros and take that one last chance to steal a look into the secret place.

Ugh. Now that I wrote all that out, I feel all wishy-washy about it again. Maybe I'll phone Sam tomorrow and talk to her about what we've decided and see if any alarm bells go off for her.

On a decidedly good note, it's Thursday again so I made it to 16 weeks; so exciting.

Wednesday, January 30th, 2008

My mom called today. She has been visiting Jack's grandma every single day for the past two and a half weeks. Jack's aunt Sarah has been there too, she's still staying at his grandma's house. The two of them have formed a kind of tag team, making sure that Grandma has plenty of visits and care. His other aunts and uncles all made another trip out to see her too even though they were all just out for Christmas, but they all live so far and had their home ties pulling, so it's just Jack's aunt who is able to stick around for the long haul. She has been travelling home on the weekends, and coming back for the week days. I asked mom how long she thinks Sarah will be able to keep this up, and mom said that it sounds like she's going to do it as long as she needs to.

I'm so glad that mom is close enough to help out a bit. It's a heavy load for Auntie Sarah. Her husband is retiring this year, and is in the midst of making the necessary changeovers for the company he works for. Mom said that Sarah hasn't been complaining though, and was even joking that it was good timing with her husband Roy being so busy, now she has something to keep her busy too.

I asked her if there was any possibility of Grandma going home to her own house and she said that they just weren't sure yet. She said these first weeks and months will show the most progress and it's still too soon to guess how much improvement we can hope for. Grandma's speech has been improving daily and she has been up and walking with a walker. The doctors said that this is a really important part of her recovery, but that going home isn't something they see in the immediate future. From what they said, Mom figures that these next few months will be full of plenty of hard work. If anyone is up for the challenge, it's Jack's Grandma.

Mom says that one of the hardest parts is that Grandma has been feeling guilty for being a burden. She said that often strokes will make people feel more emotional than they normally would be, and that this seems to be the case for Grandma. Each time Mom arrives to visit, or to care for her in any way, she cries and says that she doesn't want Mom to feel like she's obligated to help out. Mom said finally this past week; she told Grandma that they needed to chat. Sarah was gone for the night and Dad was at home watching hockey and it was a quiet evening at the hospital. Visiting hours had just begun, and it seemed the perfect opportunity to talk to her.

Grandma was already a little teary, so Mom told me she just jumped right in and said, "Lois – I want to tell you how much I have appreciated you letting me come."

Grandma seemed confused as to why Mom would be thanking her, so Mom used her momentary silence to continue, "You have always been such a lovely example to me. I have been inspired as I have watched you over the years, to want to be the kind of grandmother that you have been. I watched the way you welcomed Jack into your home when he was just a teenager, all those miles away from his mom and dad. It was a blessing to him to have your influence and guidance during his first year away from home, and it was just so typical of you to open your door to anyone that Jack brought home during that year, including my Anna.

I don't think that anyone has ever walked in the front door of your house and not felt welcomed. At church, you've always been the one, seeking out the young moms who are overwhelmed and over tired, and inviting their little ones to climb all over you. As a matter of fact, I don't remember the last time I saw your lap empty when there have been children in the room!" Here, Mom said that Jack's Grandma finally allowed a smile, so she pressed on, "You always have your arms out, your door open – and cinnamon buns in the oven. You model hospitality, and generosity. Lois, Anna has told me about your late night phone calls when you know that Jack has a late shift and Anna's at home alone. She told me how you turn her focus from her own loneliness to the company of God – and you ask her what she has been learning lately – before excitedly sharing with her your most recent discoveries. You are just the kind of woman that I watch, and that I wish I could become."

At this, Grandma began to cry a little again, but Mom felt like she couldn't leave without letting Grandma know that her value wasn't dependent on the things she had done, or what she could contribute by the work of her hands. She wanted to impress on Grandma that her influence went well beyond the cookies she baked, and the beds she made ready for company. Mom said she stayed for the full two hours that were allotted for visitors, encouraging Grandma to see that God had not forgotten her in her weakness – He had a purpose and a plan, even amidst the brokenness of this situation. She challenged her to look to Him and to ask Him – in these days – what He required of her.

Friday, February 1st, 2008

Anxiety again today, out of nowhere.

I feel like I'm nestled nicely into my second trimester, my belly is growing, and my morning sickness is still holding on, as much as I'd like to be done with it. It's not horrible like some of my friends have had, but it's nagging and exhausting. You'd think all these symptoms together would be enough to give me peace, but they're not.

Jack and I actually got in a fight about it. He's so tired of my constant agony – he wants me to sit back and enjoy my pregnancy, to sip in the sweetness of this moment, rather than ruining everything with my worry. I told him that I am enjoying it, but that I can't help but worry when my only other experience with pregnancy ended so sorrowfully. His 'get over yourself' attitude seemed cruel in my vulnerability, and I told him so. We went back and forth until I could tell that he was tired of even talking to me, and to be honest, I was pretty tired of talking to him too. That's rare for us.

Jack and I seem to be lovers, not fighters. So far, it hasn't been that hard to cope with our differences and love seems to win over harsh words; and tenderness over coldness. We've always both been on the gentle side with each other; peacemakers, companionable, comfortable, easy going...each giving in when it seemed more important to the other; finding out we agree on more than we disagree on and that the middle ground isn't too difficult to travel on. My passion grounded by his realism, my artsiness made more beautiful by his practicality, my frustration reined in by his ability to see all sides of a situation. His sociableness stretches me, his generosity teaches me and his work ethic inspires me. I like to think that we're a perfect match. I'm grateful for that... but tonight, we had a fight.

In those moments, it felt like he was out to hurt me, and I felt like I just wanted to hold my stubborn little body away from him. There was a dissatisfied sadness looming over us and he went to go soak in the tub. There was a little battle in my own heart at that moment when I was about to learn a valuable lesson.

I felt like going; getting out of the house, showing him how frustrated I was... running.

But I also felt...vulnerable, like I wanted him to hold me, and like I needed our togetherness more than anything... staying.

In that moment, I decided to let love win. I flung open the bathroom door and jumped into the tub with all my clothes on and held on with all my might. Poor Jack... he laughed at me. But in that moment, I learned that I needed to let go of the personal space that I was holding on to. I needed to let go of the things that divide and cling to the things that unite. While I know that that doesn't mean the resolution or the end of an argument – my anxiety is still going to drive Jack crazy, and his lack of compassion is going to sting at times, but I found that even in the midst of a discussion I need to check my heart and make sure that love is always winning - not me - but love. I can't care if I look desperate, or crazy, or if I lose face - there's no score.

And so what if I am desperate? There are some things that are worth being desperate over, and my magical marriage is one of them.

Sunday, February 3rd, 2008

Oh, sadness came to my house today. It's dumb, the things I want to hold onto.

Our old computer crashed.

We took it into the shop and the guy kindly fetched as many files as he could. He put them all in a nice easy to find little icon on my desktop and told us that was the best he could do. I was pretty happy with that, considering I had a lot of pictures, and it looked like he had managed to save them all. I didn't really think about the things he hadn't been able to save... until today.

I had a queer little ache in my chest. I needed to listen to a song that Julie had sent me. This song ministered to me in my sadness when I lost Tuesday - it spoke aloud the names of God My Provider, My Healer. I turned on my new computer to find it to play again.

My song lists were gone.

My song list titled, "Baby Tuesday"...Gone.

I feel it a poignant loss.

The lists were comprised of a wide variety of songs... of comfort - of haunting melody - of healing. There were songs that were mainstream, songs with children's voices, songs that meant something - only to me - in those dark hours. The list as a whole might make you wrinkle your brow in confusion, it seems so strangely put together... but it was meant for me. Oh, Jesus, just that little bit of physical comfort for me to hold onto - that list of songs that I'll only remember half of - and maybe never be able to find and put back together the way I put them together in the dark days. I just wanted that...

I never realized how hard it would be to lose a little piece of comfort. A piece that would have always reminded me of when my Father met me in my sadness and through the sounds of notes, chord progressions, rhythms and beautiful words - becoming the groans of my spirit; ministered to my broken heart through the music of His servants.

Tuesday, February 5th, 2008

Julie phoned me. Since we both work strange shifts, sometimes we'll just call each other in the middle of the day and hope we catch the other at home. Today was one of those days.

I could tell by the sound of her voice that there was something wrong, so I waited for her to start talking. Phone conversations can be so rough; I wished again that we lived closer. I wished that I could be in her tidy kitchen, pouring us each a cup of tea with that blue teapot from Christmas. But, we make the best of what we've got, and so I nudged her quietly with my voice – and asked her gently what was up.

They had lost another little baby at work. She said it was almost the same scenario that she had told me about at Christmas time. There was a family expecting their second child. This time it was a little girl, and again, the doctors had already told the parents that the little girl's condition was incompatible with life.

Today, Julie said, was the day for that little girl to be born. Her family had opted for a caesarean section because of her condition. Julie was the supervising nurse and she knew that there would be no escaping the heartbreak of this shift, so she said she fairly gritted her teeth, knowing what was coming. She said that she was abrupt with the family, making every decision by the book – serving them guardedly and without compassion.

But they hardly noticed her.

They had made plans with the hospital to have a private room where they had brought in their own photographer to take family photos. The child's grandparents had flown in, and Julie said there was a celebratory air as the mother was wheeled into surgery. After the surgery, the baby was examined and her diagnosis confirmed by the specialists at the hospital. The doctors didn't want to waste any of the precious moments that the family was to have with their daughter, so they wrapped her snugly in a soft pink blanket that one of her grandmothers had brought, and put her into the arms of her daddy.

I could hear the groan of pain in Julie's voice as she forced herself to continue, "I get it, Anna. Finally, I get it."

The father had beamed as he brought his little girl into the private room to meet her family. Their older daughter squealed, excited to meet her little sister; the grandparents admired each tiny toe and curling finger, in low voices noting the family resemblances in the child who had brought them all together. Amidst the tears and the laughter, the soft spoken photographer delicately captured each meeting, and tender kiss.

Finally, after what seemed like forever, the mother had been wheeled in from surgery. The Father gently lowered his daughter to his wife's side so that he wouldn't disturb her incision, and Julie said that in that moment she was shamed for her lack of compassion towards them. The mother kissed the baby's misshapen head and as Julie turned to leave, she caught the words of blessing that she spoke over her daughter. "You're worth it."

Julie was now crying softly into the phone and I could only listen as she told the story that had unfolded that day in a city hours away as the ripples of a fragile baby's life extended and changed hearts beyond what her family would ever realize.

The family had declined invasive medical interventions, and had instead decided to enjoy what moments God would measure out for their little one. As it turned out, it wasn't long before the little girl began to lose her color. The grandparents, after their whispered words of parting, took the older child out so that the mother and father could say goodbye alone. They could tell that the time was getting short.

Julie said she had lost her impulse to run. She realized as she sat at the nurses' station and prayed – that something important was finally breaking through her subconscious – the sanctity of life. There was a fragile balance between two extremes. This family had neither thrown away what they had been given – nor had they held on so tightly that their baby's life was torn from their hands. Instead, in a manner of complete surrender, they had held their hands with their palms open – allowing the Creator to give... and to take.

When the little girl died – Julie found in herself what it was that made her want to become a nurse in the first place. She kept her eye on their door, guarding it closely to give them the time they needed before they surrendered her little body. When they called her in, she cradled the tiny bundle in her arms, and told her parents what a gorgeous daughter they had brought into the world. She asked them if they would like a lock of the baby's hair and when they said yes, she clipped some of her silky black locks and put it in a little envelope for them. Together, they made imprints of her hands and feet, as the photographer took more photos of these last moments together.

When her shift ended, she stayed with them, watching the mother for signs of pain or complication and making sure that they had what they needed.

Julie said that when it came time to go, the mother and father thanked her for her compassionate care, not having noticed her hardness prior to the baby's birth. Their gratitude made Julie even more ashamed of her earlier behavior. They told her that their daughter's life, both the nine months before she was born, as well as the brief hours after her birth had been such a gift – they were only sorry it was over so soon.

Julie then asked if they had chosen a name for their little girl. They told her they had, and that her name was Shiloh which means 'His gift' because, they said, she most certainly was.

Thursday, February 7th, 2008

Today I'm 18 weeks pregnant. I have gained seven pounds, and today is the day that I get to record that I'm sure I felt the baby kick! There have been a couple of times where I wondered if maybe I might have felt something, but it was always so soft and tentative. I could never be sure if I felt what I thought I felt, or if I had just imagined it all. Today, I was soaking in the tub, and as I lay there, tempted to fall asleep in the warm water, suddenly I felt a tiny thump. I almost held my breath, hoping that I would feel it again. Sure enough, only seconds later, it happened again! I put my hand on the outside of my abdomen and it happened a third time. This time, I felt the tap not only from the inside, but from the outside too!

Jack is at work, but the minute he gets home, we're going to go on baby watch and hope that our little one feels like doing gymnastics again!

Only two more weeks until we reach the halfway mark! Baby, I sure love you, little person. Sometimes I feel my heart seeming to expand right inside my chest. I try to picture your face, your features, your personality... and I find I lack the imagination. I often think that I wish that God would have created women with a little window to the womb - so I could watch you and see that you're **ok**... but then I know that even in this silly detail, it was never beyond God's capabilities - He just had another, better idea. His idea was that you would be formed in the secret place. And so, baby - grow - in your little nest. Mama will take this flying leap of faith with you and trust that God - who loves us both so much - will hold us in the palm of His hand as we fly.

Saturday, February 9th, 2008

Another weekend at work; and I'm exhausted. At least Jack is working too, I hate being at work if Jack is off. I'm stealing a tiny break to write in my journal.

Yesterday Jack finally got to feel the baby kicking. We were lying in bed and after he had his hand on my belly for at least a half hour with no luck, we rolled over to go to sleep. I had my belly pressed up against his back and suddenly we both felt that tiny, faint little thump as our little one wiggled between us. Jack laughed out loud and said, "Hey, pipsqueak!"

Oh, and I forgot to tell you, Sam called yesterday! She booked our ultrasound for the 28th. I'll be 21 weeks along; more than halfway.

I asked Jack if he wanted to find out what flavor of baby we're having. He looked at me like I said the craziest thing he had ever heard in his whole life and said, "Of course not!"

I want to.

I didn't want to admit it to Jack since he felt so strongly about it, but a very big part of me wanted to have that intimate piece of knowledge about our baby. I'll never get to know if

Tuesday was a boy or a girl – and I feel like I don't want to wait a minute longer to find out what this little one is.

But I will... for Jack.

Essa just curled up beside me and brought me her favorite Archie comic book. She loves when I make up silly voices for Reggie and Big Moose. Yup, believe it or not - this is my job. I love it.

Monday, February 11th, 2008

My midwife appointment was a bit of a rush today. When she measured my uterus, she said it's just under my belly button. I told her I have started feeling some movement, and she said that's always a comforting stage to get to. She told me that there still might be quiet times when baby is sleeping or quiet for a time and that's nothing to worry about. She suggested that as I get farther along, it's not a bad idea to take a few minutes break, have a snack or some juice and just listen to my baby and count the kicks. Sounds like my idea of heaven.

She had already gotten the results back from my lab work and she said it all looked perfect. It felt like there were no questions for once, and so before long, I was on my way.

Thursday, February 14th, 2008

It's Valentine's Day. Jack and I have never been much for holidays – and Valentine's is no exception. We usually kind of ignore it, but then tonight, Jack came through the door with flowers. I had no idea the man knew how to buy flowers. He had put his things on top of them in the truck when he drove home, so they were a little squished, but still so pretty. I asked him why he was suddenly celebrating Valentine's Day and he said they weren't for Valentine's Day, he bought them because I only have one more week until I'm half way through the pregnancy.

I don't care why I got flowers... I just like them.

Sunday, February 17th, 2008

At church this morning, the pastor spoke about grace.

It was freezing cold outside, and I couldn't get warm. Jack pulled my chair closer to his and kept his arm around me, and I kept my jacket on, zipped right up to my chin. I just sat and cried, through the whole service.

Call it hormones, call it being too tired, call it hitting too close to home, I don't know what was up with me this morning. It's just this whole idea about grace. Grace has always been pretty easy for me to extend. I get that you're sinful, petty, wrong, angry, hurting...because I've struggled with those things too. So, to extend grace isn't a huge stretch for me. What hit me from the get-go... was my own neediness.

It was like I got a flash of truth - that I require so... much... grace. Will I require so much that Jack will run out? Will I be so in need of grace from my children that I will stretch them too thin? Will my sister and parents get tired of constantly extending grace and expect me to finally learn? I was overcome with grief.

Yeh - Jesus so freely extends grace -and I'm grateful. But I sat in my shame and sorrow, knowing that as long as I live in company with other human beings - I will be *needing* grace extended to *me*. And I don't know how to be better. I don't know how to live to a higher standard - try as I might. I don't know how to hide my own heart - and display a less fragile, more perfect one.

The only thing I guess that I'm capable of, is to extend even more grace... right? Where grace can no longer be extended to me - I need to extend more grace to the person who gets - understandably - irritated or angry with me for my own foolishness.

Could it be that the solution to needing something so desperately…is to give it more lavishly?

I need to go, Jack and I put on our sweats as soon as we got home and now we're having popcorn and orange juice for lunch. It's the perfect day for staying inside, turning up the furnace, and playing Scrabble.

Thursday, February 21st, 2008

Darling Baby Pipsqueak,

Did you know that at some point this week, you crossed an imaginary line? It's the line in pregnancy that defines you as a baby.

Maybe right now, you are looking down at your little toes, wondering how in the world you could be more of a baby because you hit 20 weeks than you were at 19 weeks. It's something I've found myself wondering too. Because I lost Tuesday at 13 weeks, it's as though to some people, that little person didn't really exist. Maybe it's the legacy of abortion in our country – people are uncomfortable talking about those babies who die before that imaginary line of personhood is crossed. There was no need to document Tuesday's little life. I guess - because, in a way – Tuesday hadn't crossed enough of those imaginary lines.

For whatever reason, God took Tuesday Home early, before those lines got a chance to be crossed. It's not something I'll pretend to understand – but as the Author and Finisher, He makes no mistakes in the giving and taking of life. Maybe a small part of it was to make me aware of the disparity in our compassion for losses at different stages. I don't know. I do know that when I lost Tuesday – I told God I was so grateful to Him that baby was far enough along that just maybe, I could see the little person who I had wanted so much to mother.

Once the doctor assured me that our baby would be 'whole' – I asked if there was any possibility that I would see the baby. The doctor told me how little our baby would be, and said that it was entirely possible that I would miss the baby altogether. From that moment on, I asked God to help me so that I wouldn't miss the chance to see. Tuesday was tiny. Like the size of the top of my pinky finger tiny. I could see tiny (and by tiny, I mean thread-like) arms and legs... just incredible. Tuesday's little eyes were there – but seemed in the wrong place still – y'know what I mean?

I think it was a very special gift that I got to see that little person's sweet frame at that very precious, tender stage of pregnancy.

I felt such a fierce protectiveness after Tuesday was born, that I didn't want to even show Jack. When he asked me if he could see baby's body – I was terrified – that he would say the wrong thing and crush me – or that he wouldn't be tender enough. It was a huge leap for me to be able to show him – in silence – our little one. He looked at Tuesday and then he said, "It's amazing what happens in just a few short weeks, isn't it?" And it wasn't the wrong thing to say.

We got to share our tiny child together for just those few minutes... and I'm glad I trusted him.

I know from what I've read that it can be very hard for mamas to go through miscarriage and never ever get to see the little person – I prayed constantly from the time I knew I was going to miscarry until Tuesday came, that I wouldn't miss that little body. I researched on the internet so I would know how big baby would be – from the ultrasound, we knew Tuesday was measuring right at 13 weeks. God was gracious, wasn't He? I have no doubt that each and every one of our baby's days have been ordained by the Creator - and that He has a purpose and a plan – even in their home-coming... Baby Pipsqueak, I just hope your home-coming happens long, long after mine.

I'm glad that I got to keep Tuesday for 13 weeks – even if the entirety of that little life was lived inside me, and even though the ache of the loss still makes me cry in my sleep all these months later while another little one grows. And as you cross each little line, I'm so glad that those lines of personhood are imaginary, including the one you crossed this week, baby Pipsqueak.

There *is* a day that you became a person - and that day was the day that you were conceived. Just as Tuesday became a person from the moment of conception. From that day forward, you were a distinct person - carrying your very own code of DNA - different from Tuesday's - your own unique blend from your daddy and me.

Throughout the days and weeks that passed since the moment you were conceived, you passed many milestones - developing a beating heart, all your little organs growing and maturing in your little body, eyes to see with, ears to hear with... little fingers and toes stretching and forming and getting stronger by the day... bones hardening, skin strengthening - becoming a little person who is a little less dependent on me and more ready to be born and begin to breathe air.

You didn't magically become a person at any one of those milestones, you just got a little bigger, a little stronger, a little tiny bit less dependent (though obviously, you still need me...) But, from day one - you were your own distinct little individual - my baby.

So, go little one, grow and cross those imaginary lines. But know that not one of them determines your personhood or the value of this incredible gift we've been given with your life. May your little life - in each day and every moment - be used by the Giver of life - for His perfect purposes.

Tuesday, February 26th, 2008

Lately, I have been a hormonal mess. I wish I could explain to Jack that I'm as perplexed as he is about my ever changing moods.

Today at work, one of Nikki's big brothers showed up with his wife and Nikki's tiny niece. We all tried to tease and love that little cherub out of her mama's arms, but she would have none of it. Her eyes were already pink from crying - which just added to her charm – and I couldn't help but touch her sweet little cheek and try to softly bribe a smile from her. All she could do was hold up her tiny hand to ward me off and snuggle her face deeper into her mama's neck to let me know that my advances were not welcome.

I felt like she was a kindred spirit; like I knew just exactly how she felt.

And so, in light of my mama's absence, I will choose to take my cues from that little pink thing - not yet two years old, and in the moments of weakness and inability to be a normal, functioning, social being - I will hold up my hand in surrender and snuggle my face deeper into my Father's neck and allow the comfort of His arms provide the solace that I so desperately crave.

Isn't God kind? He doesn't berate me for my irrational, hormonal state - He created me to be just so... Maybe my weakness allows me to be more easily used. Maybe my easy tears allow for communion with my Savior. Maybe as I progress through this pregnancy, I'll learn to let the back of my throat show when I laugh and let my tears show when I cry. And maybe that will be ok.

Wednesday, February 27th, 2008

Want to hear how crazy I am? I'm bitter that it's a leap year because in some strange way, in my mind, that adds a day onto my pregnancy.

I told Jack that, and he looked at me with a twinkle in his brown eyes for a long minute, like he wanted to laugh at me, but was exercising an extreme amount of self control before he finally said, "That's it! We need to get away!"

We're in the truck right now as I scribble away in my journal, on our way to the canyon. We got some crazy warm weather this week, but it'll still be frigidly cold in the mountains. I'm wearing the little spikes Jack got me for my hiking boots because he's worried that I'll fall with my tiny belly already making me more awkward than I normally am. I packed some soup in a thermos, and already my soul feels fed, just looking at the changing scenery out my window as we drive.

We have hardly spoken.

I turned to him, "Jack?"

"Yup?"

"I love you."

"I know."

"No, Jack, I like—love—love you."

"Like—adore?"

He grinned at me cheekily with the chewed up lid from his coffee cup still in his mouth. (I wonder what mineral deficiency makes him have to chew on everything?)

"Yes. I adore you."

"I know."

And since then, silence; companionable, warm and right.

I use to wonder if maybe Jack should have married a girl more like him; someone a little more quiet and steady. I use to worry that he'd figure out how annoying I can be, and be disappointed with his choice.

I realize now though, that ours is a marriage whose delicacy belies its strength. I will always be the one with the bullhorn declaring my undying love. He will always be the one quietly living it. There will always be that beautiful give and take, the stretching without tearing, and the bending without breaking. Jack and I have secret powers that make our delicate marriage stronger than iron.

You wanna know my secret power? It's potent, and comforting, and it makes me feel secure in the one task that I know I can do better than any other woman on the planet.

My secret power is that no one could ever love that man as much as I do.

And so I bask in our silence, knowing he loves me, and I most certainly adore him.

And all's right with the world.

Thursday, February 28th, 2008

I just walked in the door from my ultrasound and need to sit down to capture a bit of what today was like. Jack came with me, and I'm so glad he did. I'm not sure that I could have driven with my bladder that full. They didn't make us wait long because we were the first appointment of the morning. They made Jack wait outside for the first bit, and I couldn't see anything either because they had the screen pointed away from me. Once the tech was done all the measurements and looking for everything they look for, she called Jack to come back for a little peek.

Oh my heart!—we have a cute little baby growing in there. The first thing I saw when the she put the wand on my belly was a sweet little spine. In the next instant it was like the screen turned or something and we could see our baby's profile and a sweet little beating heart. We saw arms and legs – even fingers and toes. I'm sure that I saw the baby wave at me.

We told the tech that we weren't interested in seeing the sex of the baby, so she did her best to avoid that area. I sneakily looked as closely as I could, but I got nothin'. Those ultrasounds are miraculous, but still black and white and pretty grainy... I can't wait to see our wee one in full living color. This taste today just reinforced to me that there is a tiny person inside me who is making those little jabs and rolling movements. There's a tiny person who belongs to Jack, and to me – and who owns our hearts so completely.

Seeing our baby reminded me just how incredibly long the next 19 weeks will be, until our little one will be ready to be born. Baby already looked so perfect, and in my impatience I feel anxious to hold our precious newborn in my arms. But I know that it's not yet time, and so I'll swallow the overwhelming anticipation and daydream the rest of the day away – dreaming of those tiny limbs attached to that miraculous body – surrounding that determined little heartbeat.

While we were driving home, I was silently reveling in the afterglow of what I had just seen when Jack turned to me and in complete seriousness said, "I couldn't see a thing on that screen, could you?"

I burst out laughing. Here, today was an absolute miracle to me – and it was just utter confusion to Jack. I'm glad we bought the DVD. I'm going to make him watch it with me again tonight and point out everything he missed.

Friday, February 29th, 2008

I'm so grumpy today. Jack joked with me that I shouldn't take leap year so seriously. It's not just that February feels impossibly long, it's that I woke up in the foulest mood imaginable. Jack left his radio alarm on while he showered and it irritated me like it never has before. I burnt my toast and smashed my toe into one of the table legs. Jack spilled juice yesterday and he cleaned it up, but then today I noticed it had splashed all up on the cupboards and it's all dried on there and gross. I wasn't sad, or emotional – I was on edge, and angry.

And all the while I let the anger wash over me, a voice whispered softly to my heart that I was over reacting.

But, sometimes I don't feel like wearing Jesus. I feel like taking Him off - like a coat - and leaving Him on the rack so I can roam more comfortably in my own misery. I can be rude or grumpy - and forget that He would pull my heart towards kindness and grace. I can be quick to anger, holding a grudge and forget that He would have me lay down my rights. I can wallow in my own self-importance and forget that He thinks other people are important too.

Saturate me, Lord - so that You soak into the very fiber of my being. Don't be a surface garment that I can carelessly toss aside - change me from the inside out. Forgive me, Jesus - for my thoughtless pride, and consecrate my little life - For You.

Monday, March 3rd, 2008

Today was interesting.

I went to work in the morning, and Essa was glued to my side all day. She kept getting my purse and her jacket and bringing them to me, so finally I gave her a little snuggle and asked in her ear, "Do you wanna come on a date with me?"

She nodded her head against me while her arms still clung around my waist, and I smiled, enjoying the way my belly is beginning to stick out and make room for itself, even when I'm hugging someone.

I told her to wait till the end of my shift and then I had a surprise for her. My promise seemed to work to put her off a bit, and she managed to get all her cutting done for the new quilts that are getting sewn up this week.

As soon as we had cleaned up from supper, my shift was over and I grabbed Essa by the hand and told her it was time to go. She grabbed her jacket and mittens and the huge, hilarious fake fur hat that Megan bought her for Christmas that Essa loves unreasonably. As we pulled out onto the slushy road, she changed the radio station and I asked if she wanted to know where we were going.

She nodded excitedly and I started to second guess my idea of bringing Essa to my writing class. I wrinkled my nose and glanced at her and said, "I hope it's not boring for you, but

I'm bringing you to my writing class. What do you think? Do you think that'll be fun?"

She clapped her hands, her almond eyes shining, and I could tell she was glad to get out of the house with just the two of us. I stopped at a drive thru on the way to the high school where we have our class and got us hot chocolates.

When we got there, Ryan and Kevin were already working on their homework in the back of the room with Mr. Henry, Les was pulling into the parking lot, and Lorraine was pulling off her snow boots and shoving her feet into the bright pink slippers she had brought to wear. Essa and I pulled off our wet boots too, and Essa clutched her hot chocolate as we made our way to our seats.

Mr. Henry stood up when he saw us coming in and smiled when he saw Essa. He welcomed her so warmly that she was grinning from ear to ear, and I knew that she would have a good time.

For a writing class, Mr. Henry sure uses a lot of discussion. At the end of every class, he always reminds us that we're free to bring something that we've written to share, or we can bring a small piece that someone else had written – and we can discuss it as a class, figuring out what it is about the piece that grabs us – and moves us. There are no restrictions on what we can bring.

One time Ryan brought the note his biology teacher had written to his mother. It basically stated that Ryan was failing and that barring a massive change in test scores from here on out, it was unlikely that Ryan would pass the course. I have no idea why Ryan brought it to share; maybe he thought it would be funny. Maybe it was the only thing he had in his backpack. Whatever the reason, he stood at the front of the class, kind of laughing under his breath while he read the scathing note, pausing for emphasis at intervals, and giving a self deprecating laugh at the words, 'impending failure'.

When he finished, Mr. Henry quietly asked him, "So, Ryan, what is it about this piece of writing that moves you?"

There was a pause and Ryan tried to laugh, but instead, his face twisted and he crumpled the note in his hands. "It makes me feel like a loser." Mr. Henry gently took the note from his hands, and so softly began to teach us, using the written work that Ryan had brought as his illustration. He challenged us to consider the impact of our words – even words that brought bad news – he urged us to tread gently. He took Ryan's note, and reworded it – pointing out Ryan's quick wit, and his bright mind. He still firmly delivered the intended message, but he ended his note by outlining the steps Ryan would have to take to pass, and pointing out the hope that remained if Ryan applied himself for the rest of the term.

That was a stirring class.

There are a few classes like that, that stick out in my memory more, and that I feel like I'm going to carry them around for the rest of my life; like the ones where Les brought the hymn 'How Great Thou Art' or Kevin brought the dictionary definition of the word, "adequate". Today's class turned out to be one of them. Today, Lorraine brought one of her poems.

She stood up to tell us what she was going to read, nervously pulling the bottom of her sweater down. She bit her lip, and to our intimate circle, she spoke.

"I suffer from depression."

I think on some level, we all knew that she suffered from depression, but to hear her say it out loud made me realize what it meant to suffer... from depression.

She told us how last year, her therapist had suggested a weekly outing that she didn't have permission to cancel on, and so on impulse one day she had signed up for this writing program.

Her husband had left her fifteen years ago, and her only daughter was away for her first year at University and she had nobody to help keep her accountable. She had gone to tell her mother what she had signed up for and that she needed to go every week; asking her mother to help her press on when she felt like quitting, forcing her to go when her depression would

102

try to keep her a prisoner of her own home. Her mother was thrilled, and told her she couldn't wait to see what she would learn.

Lorraine said that her mother had always been her constant cheer leader. When her husband had left her and she gained fifty pounds, her mother had been the one to comfort her. When her daughter rebelled and she thought they'd never have relationship, her mother had intervened and bridged the gap between the two of them.

She told us that when her mother died suddenly after our second week in Henry Dyck's community writing program, Lorraine decided to quit.

My heart broke for the poor woman, standing in front of us with the frosted hair and the uncomfortable looking sweater. The room was quiet, but for the hum of the heater, as she falteringly told her story.

Lorraine said that when Monday night rolled around though, she found herself remembering her mother's thick voice, and she imagined it prompting her to get on her shoes, and go anyway. She said it took everything she had inside her to get herself out that door, but she did it.

Lorraine's voice was almost in a whisper as she continued, "There were some weeks where the only thing I could force myself to do, was to come here. The other days, I would sit in my pajamas, afraid of the world, and too sad to participate in it. But on Monday nights, I would put one foot in front of the other, and somehow or other, I'd make it here, to listen to voices of hope; and voices that acknowledged my despair too." She smiled weakly at Kevin.

Finally she cleared her throat and told us, "Enough about my silliness, I just wanted you all to know how much you have meant to me this past year. Things are looking up, as my mother used to say, and so I used Mr. Henry's assignment of writing a rondeau to remember this moment of clarity where I can finally see what really matters.

After class, I asked Lorraine for a copy of her poem to put in my journal, and she was happy to give me one.

I wish I could record the way her eyes shone when Essa started clapping, or the way she laughed when Kevin shouted out, "Nice one, Lorraine!" from the back of the room.

Suffice it to say, it was a good night, and I'm glad that Essa was there to share it with me.

Keep Looking Up – by Lorraine Morris

"Keep looking up, Beauty is everywhere..."
I'd gone, and her voice had followed me there.
Amidst the filth and void darkness around,
They lessened the burden that I had found,
And I in humbled state heard from his lair.

Echoes of mercy now rang through the air.
Lies bonds, by sweet truth now beyond repair,
Free now, I stumbled towards that Great sound.
"Keep looking up."

How foolish I am! This truth I can bear!
Never about me, that lie's a snare.
Oh, Truth, free me from that bloodthirsty hound,
it's all about Him - His beauty abounds.
My eyes from Truth's garments, I cannot tear.
Beauty is everywhere.

Friday, March 7th, 2008

Jack and I both have the day off today. My body was just aching in the night and I must have been up about 20 times to use the bathroom. We were both bleary eyed this morning, and woke up at the same time with the sun streaming in our window. I had no idea what time it was, and I'm sure Jack didn't either. We just lay there for what seemed like forever looking at each other, until finally Jack broke the silence and grinned through the sheets he was huddled under, "Wanna kiss?"

That's why I like Jack.

Tuesday, March 11th, 2008

I took Essa with me to my midwife appointment today. Lately, it seems a lot of the other girls keep getting invited on special outings with their families. Essa is keenly aware of her lack of family and seems to make up for the biological family she lacks by reaching out to others, and creating a sort of family of her own. I'm glad that I made it into Essa's little circle of companionship, and I love to let her into ours.

Sam was sweet to Essa, asking me if it was okay to let Essa be her apprentice today. I told her to go for it, and Essa was in her glory. First I got Essa to hold my chart while I weighed myself, then after Sam palpated my belly, she got Essa to do the same. My belly is still pretty tiny, rising just above my belly button, but Essa gently fingered around it, trying to find its perimeter, and grinning proudly at Sam when Sam told her she was a natural. Afterwards, Sam used a funny looking little thing called a Pinard Horn to try to listen to the baby's heartbeat. She let Essa try too, but she told me that the baby was still a little small, and the sound was pretty faint with the horn. She tried again with the stethoscope and when she found it, she got Essa to take a listen. When Essa heard what she was told to listen for, she started waving her hand like a conductor, as she stared off into the corner of the room, concentrating on the sounds of life that flowed into her ears like a symphony.

I told Sam about the pains I have been having on the sides of my belly, and she said it's all a part of my body growing and stretching to accommodate the little one inside. It's amazing to me, that as clueless as I feel about this whole process, my body still seems to know just what it's supposed to do. I asked Sam about our ultrasound results and she said they had come in, and all looked well with no reason for concern.

When we stood to leave, she took one last look at my chart and said, "Only one more month and then we'll start your visits every two weeks, alright?"

I have no idea why that gave me such a thrill. I love going to that little purple room, and talking to someone who is as engrossed in the growth and well being of my baby as I am. Getting to the point of pregnancy where you go every two weeks seems like you're rounding some kind of bend that brings you to the home stretch.

I can't wait to meet Jack's baby.

Thursday, March 20th, 2008

Twenty-four weeks today. Jack said my maternity pants don't look quite as ridiculous as they did before. Sam told me that my baby weighs about one pound right now; funny that I have put on 15 pounds for my little one pound darling. I tried on my favorite jeans this morning, but I couldn't get them up over my thighs! Sam assures me that it's normal to put on weight all over your body, not just on your belly, but it's a little alarming to watch your body grow and change and stretch and accommodate – normal or not.

Next week at work, we have our annual Spring Sensation. Megan started organizing it when she took over as the coordinator for the Manor. Every year in the last week of March, she calls in all our volunteers and every staff member. All the residents get taken to the community center. They get a full day of activities including swimming, painting, and depending on the weather, sometimes they go outside and have a picnic. One year, our volunteers went all out and hired a bus and took everyone to the mountains for the day. This year, Nikki's mom is in charge and I know she has rented the community center and they even have the massive kitchen and they're planning on making their own pizzas.

While they're gone, the staff members and remaining volunteers do a thorough spring clean on the Manor and Workshop. We putty and paint, we empty the kitchen and scrub cupboards, we get the drapes cleaned and with Megan supervising, there is not one square inch of the place that doesn't get cleaned. Megan says the residents work so hard at the Workshop every year, they deserve this once a year party, and they love coming home to see what we've done. This year, she has met with each one of the residents about their rooms. They each got to pick a paint color and all of their walls are getting freshened up. Essa picked yellow. I can't wait to see how excited she'll be. My girl loves color.

Jack isn't working that day, so he's planning on coming to volunteer too. I mentioned it at writing class too, and so I'm hoping that maybe some of them will be able to come and pitch in too. It's such a great event.

I think secretly Jack is only coming to spy on me. He told me I'm not allowed to do any heavy lifting – but I'm sure Megan will be able to find some work for me that won't be too physical.

Friday, March 21st, 2008

It's Good Friday today. Jack and I decided to take Essa to the services at our church. I think the sorrowful melodies of the songs weighed on her tender heart a little too much. I like the somber service, but Essa cried during the first hymn and then during the second, she got her purse and went and stood at the door. Jack followed, and so then I figured I might as well too. We went for ice cream instead. It's Friday, but Sunday's coming...

Sunday, March 23rd, 2008

Indeed

Take me Jesus -
My little pennies for your coffer -
My tiny faith - multiplied by
You.

Your promises kept.
My Hope leads me home.
My eyes ever on You;
Your fingers ever leading me.
To that place -
Where clouds are parted, shadows have passed, light prevails.
He is Risen.

Thursday, March 27th, 2008

Well, our 10th annual Spring Sensation went off without a hitch. It was really great because someone donated the money to purchase new quilts for each of the residents from the Workshop. We decided to surprise them with room makeovers to match their new quilts. They had picked the paint colors, but we got them each a set of new sheets and their new quilts. Their rooms looked so awesome when we were finished. It was chaos when we got there in the morning though. Megan had a bandana covering her shiny hair and an enormous clipboard where she had each job assigned and categorized. She had the vans loading up the residents, and the volunteers arriving all at the same time. She looked like she was having the time of her life.

Once the vans were loaded, she called all the volunteers into our huge dining area and divided us all into teams. There was even a team that was going to do the yard clean up, but since there is still too much snow on the ground, she got them to chip ice off the walks, and organize and sweep out the garage. Too bad the weather didn't get the memo that it was Spring Sensation.

Lorraine, Ryan and Mr. Henry all made it, and Jack grabbed Ryan for his team that was doing the sanding, puttying and painting in three of the rooms. When pretty much everyone was assigned a job, there was just me and Megan left and she grinned at me, "I'm keeping my eye on you, girl. Jack made me promise him you won't hurt yourself, so you and I are going to do an inventory and get a shopping list together."

Each year, during spring clean, Megan goes through the whole house and makes a list of things that we need to replace, or stock up on. She counts the cups and glasses – because we seem to break quite a few of those during the course of the year – she pulls out all the pots and pans and makes sure we have all that we need to keep the house running smoothly.

I know she could have done inventory all on her own, but I was glad she gave me something that I knew I could do without hurting myself, and besides, I thought it might be fun to do it together. Megan is a machine and I figured I could probably learn a lot from following her around for a day.

After about an hour's worth of taking notes on her giant clipboard as she shouted commands to me from the top of the counter while she scrubbed out the top shelves, she asked if she could bend my ear a bit. She still had her head poked in a cupboard, and I assumed she wanted to talk to me about something work related, so I said, "Sure," not even glancing up from the notes I was taking.

When she said, "I need to thank you for something," I stopped what I was doing and started to pay attention. She didn't even pause, but in typical Megan fashion with her rubber gloves up to her elbows, she talked as she scrubbed. She told me how that night in December, she had not ever intended to talk so freely, and when her words had tumbled out unchecked, she had felt a moment of panic; she thought that she had said too much, and that I would be angry with her or add to her guilt. She glanced over her shoulder. "You didn't do either of those things. You didn't say anything. I was so grateful for your silence."

I was shocked. I had always felt guilty for not having the right thing to say in those moments that night, and the right opportunity to add to the conversation had never presented itself. Now, here she was, thanking me for my silence.

She opened the next cupboard and called out, "three more dinner plates and a new gravy boat; this one is all chipped." I scribbled while she emptied the cupboard and started to talk again.

"After that night, I went home. If you can even imagine, in all these years, Cam and I have never talked about that baby. But that night I was in the mood to talk and for once, he listened. I told him how I didn't think I could go on carrying this regret for one more year. I told him I hated myself for what had happened, and there was a piece of me that had begun to hate him too."

She told me how he didn't seem surprised, and for the first time in a long while, they sat and really talked. She said that she could hardly believe it when he said he was sorry. He said that he had often wished he hadn't spoken so harshly and without thought in those first days after she had told him she was pregnant. He said he wished he would have come home and figured things out like a man, rather than allowing her dad to take her to that clinic.

She said that they got all sorts of dirt and dust out that night, and she said it was all thanks to me opening the doors of the house of mourning that quiet night in December.

Since then, she found this program that the Crisis Pregnancy Care Center offers. It involves counseling for women and families who are suffering from post-abortion trauma. She said it has been an incredible experience to go with Cam, week after week – to realize that they're not the only ones who feel like they were lied to all those years ago when they were promised a quick fix. She paused, just the slightest pause in her manic cleaning, and said with her head still poked in a cupboard, "It's almost like the years between have melted away, and right now, I can express the words that I wish I would have had back then."

The program is three months long, and she said they'll be finished next week.

Then suddenly, she wrung out her cloth and said, "Anyway, I just thought you'd want to know, and I really wanted to thank you, for calling me when you needed me and for letting me help you. I don't know that I would have ever had the courage to go down that road again, if I hadn't watched you working so bravely through your grief."

And, without another word, she was all back to business; back to shouting out items to add to our list, and getting me to refill the hot soapy buckets and empty the overflowing trash bag.

Wednesday, April 2nd, 2008

Another month gone, and we're another month closer to summer sunshine; and our baby.

I'm beyond exhausted. The day after Spring Sensation, Essa came down with what we thought was another cold. Over the weekend it got so bad that Megan took her to emergency. They admitted her right away and Megan says that it looks like she's got pneumonia again.

I just don't get it. It seems like every time we turn around, it's another hospital admission for her. Jack and I went to go see her on Sunday after church. Jack brought her flowers again, but this time, she hardly smiled.

While we were there, the nurse came in on her rounds and she was so harsh and rude with Essa. It makes me wonder why some people choose a profession that requires them to care for others when they are obviously void of compassion. When Essa gagged on her pills, the nurse scolded her and said, "Fine by me then, if you won't take your pills – I guess I'll just have to tell the doctor that you're refusing to cooperate with me."

I was livid.

Jack took me by the hand and squeezed hard, his way of telling me to hold on to my temper for a minute. After the nurse had gone, and we had Essa all settled in again, he asked me to come out and show him how the coffee machine worked. While we walked down the hallway, he said, "Anna, I know you're frustrated, but you need to figure out how to work within their system. That nurse is going to be alone with Essa all afternoon. If you start a fight with her, it's not going to help Essa's situation at all."

Something about shutting up and taking her abuse didn't sit well with me, and I told Jack so. He told me again that I needed to try to keep the peace. Hopefully Essa would be ready to come home soon.

By the time we got back to the room, Essa was already peacefully sleeping. She looked so sweet all curled up under her blankets. Even Jack had to smile. She kept licking her lips in her sleep, and so I put some lip balm on her little pink lips, taking care not to wake her, and Jack and I slipped out.

Tuesday, April 8th, 2008

Mom phoned me today. The doctors are convinced that Grandma had another stroke in the night. They said it was a smaller one, but it was obviously big enough to take away some of the ground she reclaimed since her last one. She lost more of the mobility on her right side, her speech is more slurred and when they tried to get her up and walking today, they found that she couldn't.

Mom is beside herself.

I feel guilty, like we should be there with her. Jack talked to his parents, and they feel sick that they haven't been home in over a year. They have been planning on coming since we told them about the baby, and they booked their flights to be here for over a month, figuring they'd get a chance to stay at Grandma's and help out for as long as possible, and then coming to see our fresh bun whenever baby arrives, but their tickets have them booked to arrive July first, and that's still so far away.

I talked to Jack, and after he talked to his parents, we decided that we'd make one more trip before the baby comes. Jack has a few days off in two weeks and I can always rearrange things at work, and this way, we don't have to change my midwife appointment which is on the 15th. I'm dreading another long trip, but Jack says it'll be fun... and there's a little voice telling me that sometimes there are things more important than my own comfort.

Tuesday, April 15th, 2008

I just realized today that on Thursday, I'll enter my third trimester.

I look like I ate a little watermelon.

My midwife appointment today was exciting. We did all the usual and then Sam asked me if I had given any thought to my birth plan. I had to admit that I haven't really. Since I found out that we were pregnant, I've dwelt on the anxiety of the first trimester, and the hope of eventual motherhood... but not as much on the actual 'giving birth' thing.

Sam told me there are a lot of things to consider. She actually had a handout with some suggestions for putting a plan together. There were so many things on there that I had never thought of before, things like: a list of positions to labor in, suggestions for ways your husband can help you, choices about locations for birth, and requests for care of mother or baby immediately after birth. It had a list of supplies, things like cozy socks, breath mints, peaceful music and a camera. Just reading through it made my heart speed up. I'm making it my project to put together a birth plan by the time we get back from our trip.

When I got home, as I started reading through some of my options though, all I could think about was the night I finally delivered Tuesday.

I wish I would have had a birth plan then – it was all so scary and sad.

This time, I'll do better.

PART III

Thursday, April 17th, 2008

I went to see Essa before we left. She looks like the antibiotics are kicking in and the nurse I spoke to (a different one from the mean one this weekend) told me that she thought it was possible that Essa would be home for the weekend. I'm so glad – I hate to think of her all cooped up in a hospital room the whole time we're away.

I did Essa's fingernails and toenails before I left. I love her little feet. She picked bright blue, and she sat so perfectly still while I painted them.

Monday, April 21st, 2008

It's late and I should be getting into bed, but I can't sleep. We're leaving tomorrow for our trip. I was kind of glad that Jack had to work today so that I wouldn't have to miss my writing class.

Mr. Henry brought a short story that I'm sure I have heard before. It was the story about a bunch of British soldiers who got trapped on the beaches of Dunkirk. They managed to send a short response to their leaders who had sent them a message of hope and resolution. Their three word reply was, "And if not..."

He told us how at that time, the people of Britain all recognized the phrase and understood that the words referred to the Bible story about Shadrach, Meshach and Abednego who faced the fiery furnace for refusing to bow down and worship King Nebuchadnezzar. They said that God could save them if He wanted to, but even if He didn't, they still weren't going to bow to him or any idol.

We talked for a long time about having a shared frame of reference with those who would read our words.

Then he placed the sheet of papers he held in his hands gently beside him, and turned to ask us, "How would you finish that sentence, 'and if not'?"

I had to think hard about that.

Those soldiers were hoping for a best case scenario – being saved from their enemies as they lay trapped on the beaches. And if they were not saved – they made clear by their message that they would choose the fire over bending to what their enemy wanted to make of the world.

When my best case scenario is held hostage, do I have the courage to peek at my 'and if not'?

I find that I want to uncover my eyes – and take a good, long hard look at what I believe because if it changes with my circumstances, then it's just not good enough.

Tuesday, April 22nd, 2008

Believe it or not, it was snowing again when we left this morning. This winter has been so long, and miserable and fierce.

I almost thought we should cancel our trip, but Jack scoffed at the suggestion, so I decided to just trust him. I brought my blanket and pillow and wore my yoga pants so I could sleep in the truck. When I woke up, it looked like we were driving through a blizzard. We decided to stop for an early lunch and see if the weather would clear a bit.

I was so glad we did because I was starving. I ate a huge cheeseburger with fries and by the time we were finished, the skies had cleared up quite a bit and the sun was even out. We made good time from there and we got to Mom and Dad's in time for supper.

After supper, I was so exhausted I didn't feel like heading out again, but Jack really wanted to go see his Grandma tonight, so I bit my tongue and we got back in the truck to go to the hospital. It's only about ten minutes from Mom and Dad's and we got there just as Grandma was finishing her supper.

I couldn't believe the change in her in only three and a half months. She has lost so much weight, and it makes her look so different. Her usual prim little perm has grown out, and her white hair rises in a feathery cloud around her face.

She smiled when Jack walked in the door, and I could see the mild paralysis on the right side of her face.

Jack, being Jack, took off his slushy boots and climbed right into her bed. She chuckled as he put his arm around her and asked her jovially, "So, Grandma, were you lonesome for me?"

We had to listen carefully – her voice sounded higher and thinner; not as bright and clipped as it used to be.

"I have been lonesome a lot in this past year, Jack, but through the years, I have discovered that loneliness is only the invitation of God, and so I decided to accept."

Jack grinned and said, "Well then, that's a better offer than I can give you."

Grandma laughed, and suddenly I was so glad Jack made me come. I found a seat beside the bed and made myself comfortable as Jack helped himself to the tiny bowl of caramels that Grandma kept by her bed for just this type of event. Even now, she was ever the hostess, making sure that her visitors were welcomed and made comfortable in whatever small way she could.

He told her all about work, and the course that he was hoping to take in the fall. He told her how our baby looked like an alien on the ultrasound, and that he didn't know what color to paint the little room that we were preparing. And then, he turned to her and asked, "And what about you, Grandma – are you doing okay?"

She turned to Jack and said, "Honestly honey, at first, I was frustrated when this body," here she picked up her twisted right hand with her stronger left, "suddenly became so disobedient. But, when I talked it over with my Father, I came to the conclusion that he brought me from infancy to the independence of adulthood. If it should be in His plan to take me back to the dependence of infancy... Who am I to question Him?"

She spoke slowly, deliberately and intentionally.

"Jack," she touched his cheek with her left hand, "I'm so glad you're my grandson. You make it so easy to tell you all the important things I am learning that I want to share with you. I want to tell how afraid I was at first, of the prospect of losing my independence. I was afraid of being alone and broken. But now I realize that I am far from alone, and that my Father, knowing the days and hours allotted to me to live on this earth, is encouraging me for the sake of the generations to come; to finish well. I hope He gives me what I need to faithfully, gratefully persevere, even in this present difficulty."

Neither Jack nor I knew what to say to her. She seemed so purposeful, poised and confident.

Suddenly, the image of the soldiers trapped on the beach flashed through my mind and it was as if I heard Jack's Grandmother's fervent prayer for health – and the three words of faith that would follow it.

And if not...

We didn't stay too long because we were tired from our trip, but we promised Grandma before we left that we'll go see her tomorrow.

Now, I'm about to fall into bed and I hope that the tiny one inside will sleep too.

Wednesday, April 23rd, 2008

It's five am and my feet are just getting warm. I'm all snuggled up in front of my mom's fireplace in her silent house as everyone else slumbers on. I couldn't sleep, and so I got up and wrote my birth plan; for Tuesday.

I know it sounds crazy, because I can't change the way things already happened, but I wanted to write out my best case scenario... and if not. Grandma's words gave me the courage to see past a plan – to see the bigger picture.

I know that in some of these things, I was put through the fire, and in other things, I was spared. I wanted to put myself back in my seven day vigil; the days between hearing that Tuesday had died, and the day when our baby was finally delivered. I wanted to write from the perspective of one who doesn't know the future, but who knows the One who holds it.

Birth Plan for Tuesday

None of this is my plan, God...

My plan begins with a healthy pink babe, born in the wee hours of a summer morning; a gleeful momma and a proud daddy.

But if not...

If this is where we're to be, then God, I would love to have this baby sooner than later. Each day waiting is long and painful, while the end result remains the same.

But if not...

If we need to go through this waiting for some purpose that is beyond what I can see or understand...then God, I would love to have this baby - after our waiting vigil is over - in an uncomplicated birth at home; surrounded and covered by the love of my husband; and we can grieve in peace.

But if not...

If this birth is complicated, please give us direction and protect my womb and my body as I deliver this little one who is precious in your sight.

But if not...

If we need medical intervention, then God, please let me be taken to a place where they will understand that this little one was a longed for child... where life is valued and precious. Let them be understanding and compassionate. Let them care for my grieving heart as well as my body that needs care.

But if not...

If I'm taken to a place where they don't understand and where they don't know You, protect me, and please preserve me from needing surgery.

But if not...

If I need the surgery, God, please protect my body and preserve my womb.

But if not...

If my womb is lost, protect my life.

But if not...

If like in Daniel, I get thrown in the "fiery furnace"...the God I serve is able to save me from it, and He can rescue me from my enemy's hand; but even if He does not, I want my enemy to know that I will worship no other.

Tonight, or should I say this morning, I found a tiny bit of comfort, in my rememberings from those days. I found comfort in the fact that even as I waited for Tuesday's body to come, the baby we longed for was no longer there. Our baby was already safe at home. Nothing that happened here could change that. And, there is comfort in knowing that even then, God held me in all the if's... and the if not's.

Thursday, April 24th, 2008

Best surprise ever. Today, Jack woke me up far earlier than I wanted to wake up. He told me that we were spending a few hours in the city this morning. As soon as he said it, I knew. I knew he was going to take me baby shopping.

My mom had recommended a store that sold quality baby supplies, and so we pulled up, took a deep breath and went inside. I thought we were at least sort of prepared. We knew we wanted a crib and a baby car seat. Those were our major purchases for the day. We figured we didn't need to get everything at once, but that those two items were pretty crucial.

I couldn't believe the rows and rows and shelves of things. There were highchairs, strollers, baby proofing supplies, special dishes, clothes, diapers, garbage cans, dressers, lamps, soothers, bottles, nursing pillows and covers, breast pumps and diaper bags.

I think that maybe I am the world's worst woman because just walking around that store completely overwhelmed me. I wondered if our baby would sleep if we didn't buy a sleep sack or a swaddling blanket. I had never even considered cloth diapers, and they had five different varieties. I was embarrassed to realize that I hadn't even remembered that we'd need a high chair, until Jack reminded me that babies can't even sit up for a few months, so there was no rush.

It suddenly felt puny to be buying what had felt like were two major purchases when we walked in.

Jack was as cool as a cucumber. He picked out a beautiful crib that was reasonably priced. It was painted an antique white, and had a little piece that would swing up over the side to convert into a changing table when the baby wasn't sleeping. The room that we're making into a nursery is pretty tiny, so we thought that would help to have a change table that's a part of the crib. He asked me what color of sheets we should get, and when I shrugged my shoulders, he picked out some with funky stripes that I loved as soon as I saw them.

Then he went to where the baby car seats were. After visiting with the salesman and buckling and unbuckling several of them, he picked out the one that he said looked the comfiest. I just followed behind him, grinning like an idiot, completely unable to make a decision or to even offer a suggestion.

Finally as Jack got the boxes loaded up to the front of the store so that we could check out, he shoved me by the shoulder and said, "Go pick out a little sleeper for the baby to come home in."

This, I could do. I went over to the racks of newborn clothes and gently fingered the soft fabrics. I picked one that was sunshiny yellow – because it made me think of Essa. I brought it back to Jack, who was standing with his dolly full of boxes in the line-up. When I held it up, he cocked his eyebrow and said, "It's kind of girly, don't you think?"

I grinned back at him and said, "You should have let me find out what we were having, it's too late now, yellow will have to do."

Jack grabbed it and added it to our pile. Something about that moment felt beautiful. Watching Jack pick out and buy these things for a little one who we both so desperately loved made me see that the protectiveness of a father was being born in him as I carried our child. The love I felt for them both was like an ache in my chest. I can't believe that this incredible thing that Jack and I have is going to expand into a family.

I know that eventually we'll have to pick up more of the necessities of life with a baby, but today was a giant leap, and in my shyness, I felt like I was assuming too much as we loaded those enormous boxes into the back of our truck; and I felt like I was counting my tiny chicken long before it hatches as I tucked that soft little yellow sleeper into the side pocket of my purse and we drove home in silence.

Friday, April 25th, 2008

Today we spent the day at Grandma's house. We got the Handi-Van to bring her from the hospital on a day pass, and we met at her house with Aunt Sarah and my mom. We didn't want to overwhelm Grandma with a whole crowd, but Grandma had asked especially for my mom to be there. Roy wasn't in town and Dad had to work, so there were just the five of us. Grandma was pretty emotional being in her own house again after having been gone so long. Aunt Sarah had been a little nervous to bring her before, but when Grandma kept asking, Aunt Sarah decided to see what she could do. She had checked with the doctors, and when they said they had no reservations about her taking Grandma home for a few hours, Sarah went ahead and planned it for today.

In some ways it was good. Grandma loved being the hostess, graciously letting Aunt Sarah do all the serving. She told Aunt Sarah where to find her pretty napkins and made sure that everyone got enough to eat. Aunt Sarah had even made rhubarb pie with some of the rhubarb Grandma had stored in the freezer, and even though Grandma hardly ate, she said the pie was the best she has ever tasted.

Grandma was glad that her plants were still thriving, and she went around and inspected each one from the confines of her wheelchair. Aunt Sarah had been careful to keep the house in perfect order – with each knick knack in its place just exactly where Grandma had left it, and it obviously pleased Grandma to see her house so unchanged by her absence.

But in other ways, it wakened in us all the realization that it's not likely to work for Grandma to be on her own anymore. It was all we could do to get Grandma in the front door, I think I told Jack 40 times not to drop her; and her wheelchair wouldn't fit in her hallways. The bathroom was a feat that took the strength of both my mom and Aunt Sarah, though they managed it so sweetly and in such a matter of fact way. The obstacles were huge – and there sure seem to be a lot of them. I felt my food sticking in my throat as I imagined the enormity of the blow for her.

The reality of Grandma needing extra care brought up so many difficult, messy problems. What did Grandma want to do with her house and her belongings? How to even broach the subject to discuss her options?

We found that we didn't have to broach the subject. After lunch, while everyone was relaxing in her sunny living room, Grandma sighed and said, "I wish David were still here."

She said his name so softly – so familiarly – like it hadn't lacked any use in the last year since his death.

Without even a note of complaint in her tone, she added, "I always did like the way he would take care of me. But even now when I miss him so keenly, I can see that God is choosing to stretch me, and I'm ready to make some new plans."

She shared how she had talked to a counselor at the hospital about her options. They said that she could choose to relocate to a facility that could offer similar care and therapy to what the hospital was giving her. Her space could be her own, and it would feel a lot more like 'home'. She said it would be a few weeks before they could confirm a space and the hospital would transfer her, but that she wanted to go because she felt it would make things easier for everyone.

I was shocked when my mom gently voiced her uncertainty.

She said she wondered if maybe this decision wasn't a little premature. She wanted to make sure that Grandma wasn't being rushed into an arrangement that she wasn't ready to make quite yet. Even as Mom spoke, Aunt Sarah seemed to wake from her reverie, and added her agreement to Mom's observation.

Sarah brought up how the doctors had told them that Grandma was still showing a lot of improvement every week, and that despite her recent setback, they felt there was still ground to be reclaimed.

Grandma seemed genuinely surprised to hear their opinions, and I noticed something spark in her eye that I don't think was there before. It seemed to me like she had expected them to be relieved, like she knew she was offering them an easy out – and she was comforted when they rejected it.

She leaned her head on Sarah's shoulder – and kind of laughed her new soprano sorrowful laugh as she asked them, "So then, what do you think we should do?"

I suddenly felt out of place; like it was disrespectful to even be discussing this as a group. I wanted Grandma to be able to stay on her own – to be as effervescent and capable as ever. I wanted her to order us all around, like she had so capably done in the past. I felt like I had never seen anyone so naked and vulnerable in my life, and I was ashamed that I was witnessing Grandma in her humility. Inwardly I scolded myself for my own cowardly attitude, but I couldn't shake my discomfort, and still, even now as I write this, my cheeks are burning.

It was different for Mom and Aunt Sarah. They didn't turn their faces from the discomfort of the situation at hand. They looked at each other, like they had maybe discussed this before, but had been waiting for Grandma to ask them for their opinions. Aunt Sarah started slowly, tentatively outlining some of the ideas that she had discussed with her siblings.

Gently, tenderly, like they were delicately fingering the petals on a rare blossom, they began to talk about the future. Their reactions spoke to the value they placed on Grandma – and the honor that they laid at the little white haired woman's feet. I wanted to weep for the beauty of it.

Jack and I made excuses and left them for a few hours before coming back to help get Grandma loaded back in the Handi-Van, but the image of those earnest faces bravely discussing a drastically different future are etched in my memory forever.

Friday, April 25th, 2008

There are some big changes coming, that's for sure.

Mom came home last night and filled us in on some of what they had discussed yesterday, and my jaw almost hit the floor when Mom said, so casually, "Maybe Lois will come and live here for a while."

My surprise must have been obvious by the look on my face because Mom started laughing at me. She said that it's not something that needs to be settled immediately. She said that Grandma still needed a chance to think over all of her options, and that it looked like now, she had several to choose from. The hospital was in no rush to kick her out just yet as they had a large senior's wing dedicated to those with longer term issues. She was more concerned that Grandma obviously wanted to regain a new kind of normal that she didn't think she'd have at the hospital. Grandma was lonely for the comforts of home. I asked her if Aunt Sarah wasn't a more obvious choice, and Mom said that Aunt Sarah had offered her house too, but that Grandma just hated the thought of leaving her church and her close knit circle of friends. Mom looked at me with a grin and said, "I'm up for it, Anna." And then she added more seriously, "It would sure be a blessing to me to have that woman in my home."

She said that Aunt Sarah had confided in Mom weeks ago that she didn't think that Grandma would be willing to move to their small town, even though it's only a couple of hours away. She said that she and Roy were contemplating moving into Grandma's house and trying to renovate it so that it would work to bring Grandma back home for as many years as they were able. Mom said that she knew even in the midst of listening to Sarah's heartbreaking quest to find the perfect solution for her mother that they would offer their home to Grandma. She said it just made so much more sense because there were fewer renovations to have done and nobody would need to relocate. "And besides," Mom said with a laugh, "we're family!"

It's interesting the give and the take that are involved in this delicate process of taking care of Grandma. All sides have to sacrifice and bend and cover it all with love. There are logistics, emotions and feelings to consider. I asked her if she has talked it over with Dad and she said she had and that he was in complete agreement. I can easily imagine the two of them taking on this type of challenge.

Even if it doesn't happen, I'm glad – and proud of them - that they're willing.

Saturday, April 26th, 2008

Julie showed up today to surprise me! I was thrilled too because I have been working on my birth plan for Pipsqueak and I didn't understand a lot of the things that Sam had included on her hand out. Julie has worked in a few different areas of the hospital, but the majority of her career so far she has spent in Labor and Delivery.

Some of what Julie knows is pretty different from what Sam has explained to me. For instance, Julie said that she has never seen a woman give birth under water, and Sam said that 80% of the women who give birth at the birthing center have their babies in the tubs. Julie also says it's pretty intense. She said that at her hospital, it's pretty rare for women to give birth without an epidural or some other form of pain relief. That scared me a bit because Sam said that if we choose to have the baby at the birthing center – which is what I'm starting to realize that I want so badly – there aren't any drugs available. What if I can't cope? Sam says that some women transfer to the hospital if they can't cope with the pain, and I can't help but think that sounds a little daunting to transfer when you're that far gone.

My new addiction is watching water births on the internet. It just seems such a beautiful poignant thing – to give birth. I feel guilty watching – like I'm intruding on someone's most sacred moment, but I just can't stop myself. Sometimes Jack will walk in and I'll be in front of my computer screen with tears streaming down my face and he'll turn and walk out again.

It was fun, though, talking through it all with Julie. She said that she has been to a couple births where she felt like she needed to thank the parents for letting her be there, they were so incredible. She also said she has been at a few that, she wishes she could forget. She told me about one woman who gave birth on the grass outside the hospital last year. She had gone into labor so quickly, that she had run out of time and the doctors and nurses had to come outside to help to get her and her tiny girlie on a stretcher so that they could bring them inside.

I laughed until I cried as she told me story after story. Julie is an animated story teller. I could just imagine it all – and I kept thinking that pretty soon, all of this will no longer be such a mystery to me. Soon, I'll have my own story to tell – and it won't be the private story of sorrow that Tuesday's story is to me.

In some ways, I feel like little Pipsqueak is a tiny ticking time bomb. I know that at the appointed time, the little bomb will go off, and there will be a great deal of pain. But with that pain will come the wonder of it all – the look of agony that I have seen on those women's faces on those birth videos, replaced by euphoric rapture as they bring a tiny naked squalling baby to their chest.

It makes me feel giddy to watch them, and to imagine my own little one, rising up out of the water.

Bring it on, Pipsqueak, tick tick...

Sunday, April 27th, 2008

Julie left this morning, but before she did, she helped me organize my birth plan. For some reason, I cry when I read it.

Birth Plan for Pipsqueak

If possible, and it's not already occupied, I want to use the Lilac room at the birth center. I would also request that no students or extra observers be present. (Julie told me to add this because she said sometimes the hospital will bring in three or four students when a woman is about to deliver and they'll ask if it's okay for them to watch. She said it hardly seems fair when they do that – and that it's nice to just say it on your birth plan, and then they don't bother you when you're working so hard.)

During Labor

*I want Jack with me the whole time.

*No external or internal fetal monitor. Doppler can be used, only if necessary. (Julie says some women are strapped to the bed the whole time being monitored. She said it looks uncomfortable).

*Spontaneous rupture of the membranes. (This one is from Julie too – she said that she has seen some women go really, really fast when their water gets broken, and it becomes very difficult to cope. I think I'd rather just let my water break when it wants to).

*Vaginal exams at the request of mom only. (I love writing 'mom' when it refers to me. Julie said a lot of doctors check the mothers too frequently and it can be really uncomfortable during labor).

*I want to try using the bathtub or shower for pain relief. (Sam says that some women call warm water, 'Mother Nature's epidural'.)

*No labor enhancing medications. (Julie says it's pretty common to give the mom something to get the labor going quicker. Sam never said anything about that, so I'll have to ask her, but I put in on my birth plan just in case).

*Option of a labor ball. (This one is thanks to YouTube. I saw a lady using one and it looked pretty comfortable. I wonder if the birthing center has one?)

During Birth

*Lights low.

*Very little conversation. (Julie said she was at a birth where the doctor and the father were discussing the score from the hockey game the night before – it just seems like silence is a little more respectful).

*Spontaneous bearing down. (This one is Julie again – she said she was at a birth where the doctor kept saying, 'push, push, push, push' until finally the mom screamed, "SHUT UP". I think I'd rather not be told what to do).

*Hot compresses, support and perineal stretching to prevent tearing. (This one makes me blush, but Julie said I have to add it).

*Baby delivered onto mom's tummy. (I came up with this one by myself).

*Cord clamped and cut after it stops pulsing. (Sam's suggestion).

After Birth

*I want some time to hold the baby before we weigh and measure.

*Lightly suction only if necessary. (Sam's suggestion)

*No eye care, PKU delayed, no vitamin K – (after researching all three when Sam brought them up).

*Nursing as soon as possible after birth. (That feels very strange to write).

I asked Jack if he had anything to add and he asked if he could bring his swim trunks. I gave him a wicked grin and said, "Yes, it's very common for the fathers to be in the birthing pool with the mom when she gives birth."

He looked like he was gonna throw up. It was hilarious. I think he'll stay on dry land.

I made him a list too, at Sam's suggestion, as part of my birth plan. Julie had a ton of great ideas, and I added some that came from Sam, and some are just what I imagine will work. I'm not giving it to him until I'm in labor. Here's Jack's list.

For Jack

Jack, if you're reading this, it's because I'm in labor and Pipsqueak will soon be here. I love you so much, and I'm so glad we get to do this together. If you want to help me, but don't know how, here is a list of things to try. I don't know what will help, but these ideas didn't sound horrible to me when I was writing them down.

*Remind me to relax my lips and say: pbbbbb, pbbbbb...

*Get me to try swaying my hips.

*See if you can get me to laugh out loud.

*Ask me if I want to use the labor ball.

*Check to make sure the lights are low – and that the music we brought is on.

*Bring snacks, camera, music, chapstick and warm socks and ice water. (These are from Sam).

*Jack, if I lose hope, show me the sleeper. It will remind me how grateful I'm feeling as I write this, and our tiny Pipsqueak is still rolling and growing in my belly.

We're heading home early tomorrow morning. The sun came out the whole time we were here, and the snow is almost all melted. It feels like maybe Spring is finally here. We're going to sneak in to see Grandma tonight, one more time before we go.

Monday, April 28th, 2008

I have tried to write in my journal several times so far on this trip home, but Jack keeps swatting it out of my hands. I finally asked if he has a crush on me, and if like a school boy, that's why he won't leave me alone. I found out that he does have a huge crush on me. I guess I'll have to put this away and flirt mercilessly with the man I love.

Tuesday, April 29th, 2008

Sam thought I did a great job on my birth plan. She said that nothing has to be written in stone, and even in the birthing process, I'm free to change my mind, but that having a birth plan gives us a frame of reference and something to go by as we get ready to have this little baby.

Sam says the baby likely weighs about 3 pounds now. That's not all that comforting since I have gained 23 pounds so far (I'll be 30 weeks on Thursday).

She also told me that there's a prenatal class that's running next week. It's only two days long and she wondered if Jack and I wanted to sign up. I decided we should go for it. It lands on our off days, and it might be fun.

It feels like we're slowly getting things ready for this baby. We've got the nursery all cleared out and Jack's going to paint it next week. I can't wait to see what it looks like when we get the crib all set up.

Sunday, May 4th, 2008

Today, we ran away to the mountains.

We both had the day off, and we slept in, so missed church. The sun was out and had melted most of the fresh snow we got with that storm last week.

There's this trail we like to go on up the canyon. It's all board-walked and they have bridges built and the scenery is breathtaking. There's a 6 mile loop that we usually do if we come for the day – or there's an easier 3 mile loop that we have done other times. Today, we did the 3 mile loop and I was lagging pretty far behind by the end of it. Jack was bounding ahead like a puppy on a leash, so finally I just called out, "Go already, you know you want to." And he took off like a bullet. I meandered back to the truck and sat at a picnic bench in the sun while he ran the other 3 miles, his lanky legs taking in one stride what would take my decidedly less lanky legs three.

I pulled out our picnic lunch and my journal, and I want to record this perfect moment. The sun is creating a hot spot on the back of my head, but I'm wearing my sweater because when the breeze blows, it's chilly. I made turkey sandwiches on brown bread, and brought cranberry juice to drink. We each have an enormous chocolate chip cookie for dessert, and if I play my cards right, Jack will give me half of his. I can hear birds, water, wind and the rustle of brown foliage finally freed from the melting snow's grasp. The tiny one in my belly just woke and is giving me the most appreciated show as I breathe the fresh air and feel the sun touch my winter whitened face.

In a few minutes, I'll see Jack, grinning, running towards me like a child – out of breath, hungry and full of life.

This could very well be my favorite day.

Thursday, May 8th, 2008

What an exhausting day! Megan and I finally had our talk about work, and Jack and I went to our first prenatal class.

Megan had asked me last week if I'd like to go for coffee with her after work today, and I said yes, fully aware of the conversation we were likely going to have. She smiled at me when we sat down; her, with her black coffee, me with my mint tea. She started out with, "You don't have to make any decisions just yet, but I was wondering what you're thinking about work and your future at the Manor with this little baby on the way. You know, that arrival keeps getting closer every day."

I told her that obviously I was going to need some time after the baby was born, and that after that, I just wasn't sure what I would be doing.

I know, that feels dishonest to me too, considering the fact that Jack and I both assumed I'll be quitting my job when Pipsqueak comes. But I'm just not ready to give my notice just yet. I love my job, and even though I know the end is coming, telling Megan just makes it so final. I was totally unprepared for what came next. Megan shocked me by suggesting something I had never even considered before. She asked me if I had ever thought of bringing the baby with me to work. She said there was no pressure, but that she was really happy with the job I'm doing at the Manor, and that a baby would only add to the family atmosphere that we have there. She said if I wanted, I could try to start casually, maybe when Pipsqueak is a few months old, and see if it was something that could work.

We had taken for granted that I wouldn't be able to work when I had our baby. Jack and I had already talked about living on his salary alone because I didn't think I'd be able to do the daycare route. I never thought about bringing Pipsqueak to work with me.

I imagined Essa's face, holding my little baby – and Tina's joy – hearing a baby's babble.

I wonder if I could juggle my responsibilities at work with the most precious responsibility I have ever been given?

I told Megan I'll have to think it over and talk to Jack about it.

But tonight, there was no time to have a real discussion about it because we went to our first prenatal class. It was a riot. Jack is a horrible student. She dimmed the lights and played relaxing music, getting us to imagine ourselves focusing through labor. Jack actually fell asleep! The teacher was furious. She went on this huge rant about being supportive of your partner, and learning how to be a little bit less selfish. The angrier she got, the funnier Jack found it until I was completely embarrassed when he cracked a grin in the middle of her diatribe. In his defense, it was a pretty boring class. Most of it covered issues that I have researched ad nauseam, and that Jack has heard me chirping about for months. He has been exhausted working over-time lately and now, with getting the baby's room ready to paint. And she did dim the lights and play soothing music. What did she think was going to happen?

I asked him if he wanted to skip the last class tomorrow and he said that we can go, but he needs to grab a coffee first. What a goof.

Saturday, May 10th, 2008

Lately, I feel kind of congested and achy. I'm having a hard time breathing at night when I go to bed. Jack went and bought me two extra pillows. Now, I sleep all propped up like a queen in a throne, with pillows under my belly, between my knees and under my head. Even so, I'm constantly rearranging myself in the night to get more comfortable, and the minute I do, I need to go to the bathroom. Even so, I'm kind of in love with my belly. My belly button pops out just the slightest bit. If it rubs on anything it gets really irritated. I can't help but stare at myself when I walk past a mirror. My body is just not my own any longer. The little one who has set up residence has changed almost everything about me. I have to wear different clothes to accommodate, my breasts are bigger, my round belly eclipses my view of my feet. Honestly, even my face looks different to me, it's more filled out – and when I lean in and really look at myself in the mirror, maybe it's just exhaustion, but my eyes look different than I remember them.

Jack likes me. His big hands are always finding me in the dark at night, pulling me closer. And he has lost the ability to just walk past me in the kitchen; he has to touch me, grab my hair, kiss my head, and rub my round belly. His tenderness adds to the sweetness of these waiting days.

Tuesday, May 13th, 2008

Another midwife appointment today! Sam says that our tiny baby is breech in there! She said it's not a big concern yet, but it's something we'll keep our eye on in the weeks to come. She gave me a list of hilarious exercises to do to encourage our baby to turn head down.

First, I have to crawl around on my hands and knees. She chuckled that the perfect work for this exercise is washing the floors. She also wants me to hang backwards down the stairs. She told me it's not a bad idea to go swimming, doing some twists and turns in the water, encouraging our little one to move. There's still a lot of time though, and Sam seemed unruffled as she explained that lots of babies will turn even in the last couple of weeks before they're born. I don't think I have felt our baby doing any big somersaults lately. Hopefully if I do some of these exercises, I'll feel something.

She also mentioned that sometimes when baby is breech, it can cause some discomfort to mom. She suggested that the ache in my ribs could be caused by a tiny hard little head. Hopefully Pipsqueak will figure out how to turn soon, and when that happens, I'll feel more comfortable.

Saturday, May 17th, 2008

Let the records show that I went swimming with Jack at 32 and a half weeks pregnant. I didn't even have a maternity swim suit, but thank goodness that stores are stocking up for summer, so I found one that would work.

I was so abashed to see myself larger than life in the changing room mirror that I didn't want to go out to the pool. I ended up stalling, redoing my pony tail about four times before I gathered up my courage and tiptoed out the door with my towel firmly wrapped around my corpulence.

To my complete mortification, Jack wolf whistled at me from the hot tub.

I thought I would slip, walking so cautiously across the wet floor, with my cheeks burning. When I finally looked up, I realized that the pool was almost completely empty. There was one old man swimming laps and two lifeguards who were oblivious to us, so I forgave Jack his indiscretion; not that he cared with his four year old grin as he laughed at my painstaking approach.

The water felt frigid after soaking my legs in the hot tub. Jack swam circles around me as I made my way through the water. The weightlessness felt amazing though and I just closed my eyes and all the misery in my muscles and bones seemed to seep right out my finger tips. I could stretch without an enormous weight holding me back, and it felt good to swim leisurely from one end of the pool to the other.

Pipsqueak woke up midway through our swim and stretched mightily, but I'm fairly certain I can still feel a hard little head just underneath my ribcage.

All in all, I'd have to say that the benefits outweigh the humiliation, and maybe a little humble pie is good for a body every once in awhile, even if it does taste terrible.

Tuesday, May 20th, 2008

All the staff and residents at the Manor threw me a surprise shower today! What a shock! I got to work for my shift at three in the afternoon, and Essa met me at the door. She took my jacket and my purse like we were in a fancy restaurant or something and then Nikki took my hand and led me to the living room. Quite a few of the families of the residents came too, so it felt like there was a huge crowd. I wished I would have dressed up a little bit, I felt like such a slob in my stretched out yoga pants. Megan served cheese and crackers and Sophie had picked up a delicious cake.

Nikki's mom made the sweetest little speech to me about the journey through motherhood that I'm about to take. The blessing and excitement in her words touched me, and I found myself in tears in front of that huge group. I couldn't help but look at the journey she has been on for all these years as I thought of her four older sons, and then sweet Nikki – and now her journey into grand-mothering. How tenderly she stroked Nikki's head as she smiled radiantly at me and described the joy in the work and the inestimable contribution that motherhood gives the world.

I saw even amidst her gratitude, the selflessness that it had taken for her to raise such a happy family. I saw the sacrifices as even now, she came daily and sat in on Nikki's physiotherapy appointments, helping her achieve her goals – while granting her the independence she had requested. I saw how painstakingly she taught Nikki each new skill when she required it. And, I saw how through the consistent example of her and her husband, their boys were now raising families who had a different view of life, humanity, and their sweet little spoiled sister as she journeyed through adulthood.

I wished as I watched her that there could be a part of my birth plan that described the kind of mother I would be. Just like the written descriptions of the process of labor and birth seemed so mysterious to me, now suddenly I realized that all of motherhood was shrouded in the same kind of mystery.

I held my hands, stretched out over my stomach – like a sprinter poised at the starting line, and I found myself knowing that I would be unable. I knew then, in that moment, that I needed to lay this little one down at His feet too. Surrendering my sudden anxiety – my certain failures – and what meager resources I had to offer. I know even as I write this, that if I am to have any success as a mother, it will have to be as a result of my Jesus multiplying my loaves and fishes; because these involuntary feelings of inadequacy are undoubtedly accurate. I don't have what it takes. But I know the one who does, and He is clearly in my corner.

Essa, seeing my tears and ever wanting to comfort and console, grabbed my hand and pulled me over to my gift. They had all chipped in together and bought me a gorgeous glider chair.

I had never seen a glider chair like it before. Nikki's mom had found it at a specialty online store. They had the most unique designs and they would upholster it with the fabric of your choice. The wooden pieces that you can see are painted the same antiqued white as our crib – and the fabric is thick chunky corduroy that is a faded blue. It looks like it belongs in a sea side cottage, not our little prairie town, with its little glider footstool sitting ready to glide with it to the rhythm of the foamy waves beating on the shore.

I love it. It's so completely over the top and unexpected. Nikki's mom was almost apologetic that she didn't get me to choose the fabric or design, but she didn't want to ruin the surprise. I told her how Jack had picked out our crib, and that I knew I could never have chosen something so lovely. I was glad they had taken the decision from my hands and picked out something that feels so right.

The rest of my night was a little crazy. The party cleared out before supper, and I was on until 11 pm. Jack came over and picked up the glider at the end of my shift and brought it home. I'm sitting in it now... in our baby's room, with the crib boxes and complete disorder reigning all around me. On a hook on the door hangs a tiny yellow sleeper – a symbol of hope and the desires of my heart.

Saturday, May 24th, 2008

Jack and I both had today off work and so we decided to paint Pipsqueak's room. The floor in there is old hardwood that we sanded down and stained when we first moved in. Jack replaced the baseboards and fixed up the inside of the closet. My mom made the sweetest roman blind for the window, and the walls have been puttied and primed for a few weeks already.

Jack said I could pick any color I wanted, and I was wishing at first that we knew if the baby was a boy or a girl, but then I realized that if I don't know, I can just pick whatever color that I like, and I won't have to worry if it's a 'boy' enough or 'girl' enough color.

I picked mango.

Jack laughed out loud when he opened up the can. It's kind of a soft mango, and I think it looks amazing. We're only done the first coat and we stopped to let it dry and to have lunch. Even Jack was impressed once we started painting. It's going to be perfect.

I can't wait till we get the window coverings on and the crib all set up. My pendulous belly reminds me constantly of our state of expectancy. Sometimes I feel like I could just burst into a crazy sort of high pitched laughter, I'm so high strung. But for today, I'll just work hard feathering my nest, getting ready for my tiny chicky to hatch.

Tuesday, May 27th, 2008

It feels like my midwife appointments are piggy backing each other now. I can't imagine what it will be like when we need to go every single week.

The big news of the day is that Sam said that Pipsqueak is still breech! I guess I'll be doing more exercises, hanging upside down, going to the chiropractor, elephant walking on my hands and feet... She also suggested putting some frozen peas at the top of my belly to encourage baby to turn. We'll see – doesn't that sound kind of mean? She said it's still really early, but it's always a good idea to be encouraging baby to get into a good position for birth.

Monday, June 2nd, 2008

Tonight we had our last writing class of the year. Mr. Henry said he couldn't resist giving us one more assignment for the summer. When we walked into the classroom, in giant letters across the chalk board were the words, "I AM".

He said that writers often feel a burden to be understood, and that sometimes it can be a helpful exercise to describe to others the things that we identify with ourselves. He said if we wanted to complete an assignment over the summer, it was to write a piece about who we are. Then, he got us to come up and write on the chalk board words that would help a reader better understand us.

Les got up and wrote in uppercase letters, "GRANDFATHER".

Ryan wrote, "imbecile" and then he turned to Mr. Henry and chortled, "Did I spell that right?", Kevin wrote, "rejected", Lorraine wrote, "hopeful", Mr. Henry wrote, "curious"...

And then it was my turn. I took the chalk in my hand and felt the dust rubbing off on my fingers. And then I wrote one word, "growing". Ryan laughed and said, "You sure are, Anna! You look like you're about to pop!"

And I hope I am; growing, that is. I hope that even as my body has been growing and changing that I'll never be at a standstill in my growth as a human being either.

At the end of the class, Lorraine said she had something to share. She said that they had all noticed how fat my journal was getting, how it's splitting at the binding, and some pages are coming loose. She handed me a pretty package and said, "It's more of a mommy gift than a baby gift, but we hope you like it." She handed me a package with a card signed by everyone in the class. Wrapped in a long strip of jade silk was a leather bound journal, inscribed on the front were the words, "What Happened Next".

Ryan said that he picked the inscription. I told him I knew he was a smarty pants and he gave me his toothy grin.

What a thoughtful gift, though.

I want to tear it open and read the words that will fill the pages that are now white, blank and pristine. But for now, it will sit on a shelf untouched while I finish these last weeks in my journal from Jack.

Thursday, June 5th, 2008

Somebody cute had the hiccups last night.

Oh, little Pipsqueak, just as I thought we were both starting to doze off, I started to feel those gentle rhythmic hiccups.

I rolled over on my side and got both my hands on my belly so I could feel you from the inside and out. Hard to believe your little frame fits in that hard ball in my belly. I try to picture you all scrunched up in there and as I feel each gentle whoosh, hiccup, or kick – I remember that that is my sweet little person hiding in there.

My body has been changing, making room for you - growing, doing crazy things because you're there.

Sometimes I'm half crazed with anticipation for your arrival... and other times, like in the stillness of the evening last night, I wish I could carry you like this forever.

Today marks a unique day. I'm 35 weeks pregnant, and I have 35 days left until my due date.

I'm counting down the last exquisite pebbles of sand in this hourglass of waiting.

Wednesday, June 11th, 2008

I didn't know what to do with myself on Monday – with no writing class to go to in the evening.

We had asked Mr. Henry if he's planning on continuing next year. He said he's not sure yet – the community decides every summer what fall programs they'll offer, and the contracts are given out for one year at a time. Ryan and Kevin are still finishing their last finals, so we're all hoping that they graduate, and its sounding hopeful. Even if they graduate, they're both planning on sticking around here for the year. Les, Lorraine and I all said we would keep coming if Mr. Henry was teaching. I guess we'll just have to wait and see. Funny that what seemed a ridiculous gift from Jack became such a life line for me.

Then on Tuesday, I had my midwife appointment. Sam was attending a birth, so I met with Rita, another midwife that could possibly attend Pipsqueak's birth. Sam said they always have two midwives at every birth so that if necessary, there is a person to care for both mother, and child. I thought I loved Sam, but Rita was amazing. She was so relaxed and encouraging. She said she'd love to go over my birth plan with me just in case she's there and Sam can't make it.

We had a big talk about coping with pain in childbirth. I asked her if she thought I was a fool for hoping for an unmedicated birth. I told her that I had friends who have told me already that I'll never make it. She replied that there was no way to tell until I tried. She said that there is no shame in requiring medication – that birthing can be a very painful process. She assured me that I wouldn't care in the end if small bits and pieces of our birth didn't go exactly as planned. If I couldn't cope, they would provide the options I required, but if I wanted an unmedicated birth, she figured that with the right support, there was a good chance I could achieve it. I thought again of the women in the birth videos I had seen, gasping in agony, and pulling their babies to their chest, and wondered how our little ones birth would play out.

Would I feel like I had failed if I couldn't follow through with my goal? I continued to ask questions, biting my lip nervously before she finally sucked in her breath, sat back in her chair with her feet propped up on the bed I was sitting on and mused, "Do you want to hear an old woman ramble on about her crazy opinions on the subject?"

I nodded, smiling meekly at her, liking her warm friendliness, and knowing I wanted to hear what she had to say.

She smiled back at me and surprised me by saying, "I think there is something to be said for suffering. We live in an age where we are so blessed that we can medicate when we need to; headaches, childbirth, dentistry, fevers, surgeries... But as a result, we've grown to expect less suffering in life - and in death. We even attempt to medicate heartbreak." I had never thought about pain having any significant value before, and I wondered what she meant by it all.

She was funny, her eyes glimmering, obviously getting into something she had given some thought to. "Don't get me wrong - I've downed more than my fair share of painkillers when I've needed them – and I've dealt with the annoyance and frustration of suffering with migraines that hurt more than my natural childbirths. I've given medications or cough candies to my children... and while I understand that pain is not fun - and yes, I do try to avoid it - or seeing my children in it, some days I wonder if we're trading off something precious when we make it our goal to avoid suffering completely.

I've heard people say, 'Why would she choose to suffer like that?' almost as if it's an annoyance - when women have chosen to give birth without pain medication. More and more I'm hearing murmurs that we shouldn't allow the sick, the struggling, or the dying to suffer either. I have been hearing that euthanasia is a more merciful option than the sometimes long, drawn out, painful process of death... and I think they're wrong.

I remember when I was having my first baby. They offered me 'something for the pain' and I remember thinking - 'If it hurts me this much, I wonder how much it must hurt her little frame, being squished like that...' I felt like we were a team and that if I could, I'd like to just keep that pain that was connecting us in this little triumph of childbirth.

I don't know if death is anything like childbirth - but in my naïveté, I imagine that it is. The groaning expectancy - the emerging of a little being from the secret place where it was formed, into new territory where all of its limbs, muscles, senses have new purposes.

I guess I have come to believe that the parentheses around life on earth should be placed by the Creator. And I think that the suffering within those parentheses might just serve as the punctuation that makes that life readable. Maybe suffering exercises spiritual muscles that we might not even know that we need, until we have finished our life here..."

Then she laughed a big cackling laugh and added, "I know - I'm ignorant on the whole subject – and I realize it sounds like I'm oblivious to the suffering and pain of others. I'm trying not to be. I do believe that we need to be compassionate and merciful to the sick and the dying, as well as to the laboring, delivering mama, but rather than casting off the unwanted burden of suffering; what if we cared for and built up the suffering ones - thanking them for giving us the opportunity to serve? Encouraging them in that difficult, agonizing transition to 'finish well'...

It was my turn to laugh, and I told her, "I don't know if I like you comparing childbirth to death – is it that bad?"

"No, no, no!" She howled, "That's what I get for not sticking to the program; let's get back to your birth plan!"

After we went through each point, she asked if I'd mind if she made a copy to share with other first time moms. She said it can be hard for first time moms to come up with a plan, because they don't know what to expect. I told her about Julie and how she had helped me get it all together, and she said I was lucky to have a sister like that.

I have to admit, I felt a little cocky that my midwife wanted to share a copy of my birth plan. I had to phone Julie when I got home and she chortled at me, "Well, aren't you smart?" I told her, I guess I am.

Monday, June 16th, 2008

I'm almost positive Pipsqueak turned on Saturday. I was at the chiropractor in the morning, and then in the afternoon, Jack and I went to the pool again. Pipsqueak started stretching again, and then suddenly something that felt like a bowling ball started to travel down the side of my belly. I had to stop what I was doing and cling to the side of the pool. My stomach felt like it was getting ripped out as that tiny baby worked its way around and down. Jack swam over to me to make sure I was alright, and at first I couldn't even speak to him. He rubbed my back and asked me if I wanted to leave, and I nodded that I did. After about 30 seconds, I felt better and when I got changed, Jack said my belly actually even looks different. It feels a little lower to me and I can't wait for my appointment on the 24th to make sure that that earth shattering event was our little Pipsqueak getting into blast off position.

Only two more weeks until Jack's parents arrive!! Jack and I decided that I'll finish work when they come, on July the 1st. They're going to fly here and stay with us for a couple of days before they drive down to see Grandma. They'll stay at her house until Pipsqueak is born, and then they'll come back here. We figured it would make sense for them to take my car because if I'm done work, we can manage with just the truck, and it'll save them having to get a rental while they're here.

I'm getting really excited.

The only thing is that Mom phoned today and it looks like Grandma is finally able to move in to their house. Dad just finished having the renovations done so that their house is all wheel chair accessible, and Grandma's doing so much better than she was. They thought about bringing Grandma all the way here when I have baby, since they bought the new wheelchair accessible minivan, but they think it's just too soon, and it would be too hard on her.

I think what they're going to do is that Mom and Dad will come first, right when Pipsqueak is born, while Jack's mom and dad stay at their house with Grandma. Then when Mom and Dad go home, Jack's mom and dad will come. It's so complicated, but Jack says since when has anything that's worthwhile been easy? And I guess he's right.

But, there's a tiny bit of me that wants Pipsqueak to be the center of attention. It's so easy to get so wrapped up in our joy that I forget to bend for the needs of others. Even though I know that I'm being selfish, I find it hard to put it aside and not care that we can't have all of Pipsqueak's grandparents here at the same time.

Jack says its better this way. Our house is pretty tiny, and it might be kind of nutty around here when Pipsqueak finally makes an appearance. He figures we should send Grandma a thank you card for keeping half of the parents out of our hair at a time. He's probably right.

Wednesday, June 18th, 2008

Today we set up the nursery.

The paint was all done, but we still needed to set up the crib and get the window coverings, and put my pretty glider in there. Jack put up a wall mounted lamp, and built some shelving in the closet since we don't have a dresser. I bought a little striped rug for the floor. I enlarged black and white baby pictures of Jack and I and both our parents for the large wall right beside the glider. They look so amazing. I did them all different sizes because the ones of Jack and I were of a much better quality than the ones of our parents. Jack's mom could only get me one of his dad where he's about 2 years old, but it's still pretty cute. I think we'll have fun as Pipsqueak grows, looking at those pictures and figuring out who our tiny one looks like. I'm getting all the aunties and uncles done too, but they're not ready yet. When they are finished, the wall will be full of tiny babies who grew into the adults who love our little one the most. I think it's going to be beautiful. Julie says she's stealing my idea if she and Dane ever have a baby. I wonder if that means she's softening to the idea of having a baby. It sure would be fun to raise our babies at the same time. None of Jack's brothers are even married, so Julie's our best hope for a cousin.

Saturday, June 21st, 2008

Megan came over today with a box of gently used baby clothes. Her neighbor had been clearing out her baby things, so Megan said she picked through for anything that was in decent shape that was kind of unisex. There were a bunch of undershirts and sleepers, a few receiving blankets and the tiniest pair of woolen booties. It was so thoughtful of her to even think of me!

I washed everything and added it to my stash of newborn diapers in Pipsqueak's closet. Slowly those empty shelves are looking more homey and prepared. I want to try to make a mobile to hang over Pipsqueak's crib. Maybe Jack's mom can help me when she comes.

I find that now that the room is finished, I want to sit in here in the evenings. Jack says I'm being anti-social because there's only one chair, but sometimes he comes in with me and sits on the floor and we grin at each other across the dim room without saying a word.

I love this room.

Tuesday, June 24th, 2008

Today my midwife appointment was with Sam again. Jack came with me since he wasn't working, and it felt like we were on a date. On Thursday, I'll be 38 weeks pregnant. I have gained 28 pounds. Sam says not to worry, that usually weight gain slows down after the 38th week. I sure hope so because I feel like I couldn't possibly stretch one more millimeter.

Sam says that undoubtedly the baby is head down, and it feels like the head is already engaged. She used the Pinard horn to listen to Pipsqueak's heartbeat, and I felt like I was a pregnant momma from a hundred years ago as she used that ancient looking wooden instrument to listen to the sounds of life from within.

I asked her to show me how the baby was positioned since I have such a hard time understanding what little limb I'm feeling when Pipsqueak starts to kick. She asked me if I'd like her to draw the baby on my belly with markers. She said there are some moms who like to visualize the little one inside, and that she had once taken a class with a bunch of other midwives on belly mapping, and she had loved the sense of reality that it gave to the mothers to visualize their babies this way.

I was so excited.

It took quite awhile and we visited while she drew on my round belly. Jack sat in the corner with an amused look on his face as Sam added chubby legs, shoulders and head. When she was done, she brought me over to the full length mirror to admire her artwork.

Jack couldn't wipe the smile off his face and he said we needed to take some pictures when we get home. Sam said it was one of her better efforts and laughingly asked if we'd get her a copy of the pictures for her to start a belly mapping album for the clinic.

I didn't even want to pull my shirt back down. I could hardly tear my eyes away from my enormous round belly. I put my hand where she had drawn a tiny perfect spine, and gently pressed my flat palm against my skin. I felt the timid wiggle as a lazy Pipsqueak moved under my touch.

Slowly, I let my shirt fall, covering up the picture underneath, and let Jack take me by the hand and lead me out into the sunshine.

When the warmth and the breeze hit me, I suddenly noticed my hunger. I was ravenous. I wanted onion rings, and

Jack obliged. He says I'm just like that stereo type of pregnant women, craving salty and sweet, first starving than nauseous. It's true too; lately I find there's not enough room in my belly for what my appetite requires. I need to eat constantly all day just to keep the hunger at bay. I wonder if the little one inside has a hunger that mirrors my own?

Thursday, June 26th, 2008

I'm 38 weeks pregnant.

And today marks one year since I found out that Tuesday was gone. I found myself sitting, sobbing in my glider last night, and when Jack found me, he asked what was wrong, was I in labor, should he call someone?

No, Jack, you can't call someone.

At first, I wasn't even quite sure what was wrong – it was like my body remembered first, before my mind did. I felt teary on and off all week, and just bone weary. I felt emotional and drained; and then I remembered.

This is the week we found out. I feel like this sorrow – this grief – has been hardwired in somehow and that despite being in this season of expectant joy, Sorrow's coming was as unavoidable as the falling of the leaves in autumn, or the blooming of the flowers in spring.

It's such a tender thing – a treasure that came about because of the love in our marriage and the grace of God – that is suddenly – delayed in a way?

This year that has passed has taken away just the tiniest edge of the agony of loss, though it's still so much a part of every single day, and in its place I feel a gratitude for that little life that God sent to Jack and to me – even for such a brief time.

I am more certain than ever that our hope will be fulfilled. So, I'm sitting in my sea side glider, thinking of heaven.

Tuesday,

You won't throw stones in the ocean...
Or try to wrap skinny arms around tall trees...
You won't trap tiny crabs in seashells...
Or comb the pebbles looking for beach glass...
And yet the ripples from your little life continue to grow
and spread...
I'm so grateful for you.

I remember this whole week a year ago, so clearly. I felt the thickness of God's presence like a cloak as I moaned and wept in the hallway, and Jack came out of our room in the night and held me as I rocked on the floor. I remember not being able to eat for two days and wishing miserably that morning wouldn't come. Each day passed so slowly as I waited for my baby's body to be delivered. I remember agonizing over every day of my short pregnancy, wondering if I had done anything to cause the death of my own tiny child. I remember the humiliation I felt when the doctor told us there was no heartbeat, and I wondered how I could have been joyously carrying on with my life while my little one's heart stopped beating within me. I hated myself for being so clueless.

July third is the anniversary of Tuesday's deliverance. I remember going through every dictionary I could find. I summarized each entry until I came up with a list of definitions for the word 'delivered'. I still have it in a drawer somewhere. Maybe I will try to dig it up and save it here on the anniversary of the birth of my first tiny child.

That week is a part of my life that I will forever remember as marked by the presence of God, and yet what struck me the day after Tuesday was delivered was that God's presence had lifted. I remember waking, still grieving, still sad and broken and asking Him where He was? I longed for the thickness of His presence that I had felt while I carried Tuesday's body – and I wondered what had changed.

It reminded me of King David's Psalms – how sometimes it sounded like God had allowed His presence to be felt and other times, He had withdrawn – and sat unseen – watching the one he loved as he yearned for his Father. And so I sat and spoke into the stillness and quiet of the room – knowing He was with me still, and that despite the fact that I couldn't feel the warmth of His presence like a cloak around my shoulders – His presence was no less real.

Sunday, June 29th, 2008

I can't stand for the singing in church anymore. I sit and weep. At least I'm getting smart enough to bring Kleenex. I hope that new era of uncontrolled emotion is a result of pregnancy and not a permanent change. Tears come frequently and easily.

Monday, June 30th, 2008

Today was my last shift at the Manor. I promised everyone that I'll be in to visit lots even though I'm not working. Essa kept trying to steal me away all day, and I'm sure I spent half of my day with her joined to my hip. We have plans to take her out to lunch when Jack's parents come; they really want to meet her. I think she's nervous about me not being at work every day though.

Megan hired a couple of girls from the high school to work through the summer, so I have been training them this past week. She said that gives her some time to find someone to fill in for my whole maternity leave. She said she wants to make sure I know I'm not replaced.

I love that woman.

When I got home from work, Jack and I got the room in the basement all ready for his parent's arrival tomorrow. I'm nervous. I picked up a ton of groceries and I have frozen meals in the freezer too, just in case. I have seen them so rarely and

I want so badly for this visit to go well. Their flight arrives at eleven in the morning. We're planning on going to the Canada Day parade in the city with them when they get in. They'll be exhausted, but they said if they sleep right away, it'll take forever for them to get over their jet lag. Jack is fairly bursting with excitement. Jack's mom said they're bringing a surprise. I wonder if it's something for the baby?

I feel completely overwhelmed with life this week. I'm not sure if it's the emotion and drama of being in the last weeks of my pregnancy, or if it's the excitement of Jack's parents coming, or if I'm trapped yet again in my week long vigil as I remember those days waiting for Tuesday to be born.

Tuesday, July 1st, 2008

Happy Canada Day!

It's almost midnight and I can't sleep. I'm curled up in my sea side glider in Pipsqueak's room. Jack's mom and dad went to bed hours ago, and Jack's fast asleep too – but for whatever reason, my exhausted body won't let sleep come to me, so I came here to write about our day.

We went to the airport at 11, knowing that it would be a bit of a wait for them to get through customs, but as soon as they came into eyesight, we found out their surprise – Jack's little brother Aaron came with them! We thought he was going to stay home, but apparently he was itching to see his big brother and his new niece or nephew. Plus, he hasn't seen Grandma in so long and they knew she would love to see him again, so they decided to surprise us by bringing him along. Jack couldn't stop laughing when he saw Aaron. And you should have seen Jack's mom's face when they walked through those gates. She fairly threw her bags on the ground and ran to us. Jack's dad grinned at her exuberance and held himself back just the tiniest bit before throwing his bags to the ground too, and picking his son up off the ground. Jack's mom knelt down right in the airport and thanked Pipsqueak for waiting for Granny to come and Pipsqueak rewarded her with a nice big thump. Jack wrapped Aaron in a big bear hug, and then

Aaron rubbed my belly just exactly how Jack would and kissed my cheek, asking if his big brother was taking good care of me.

I'm so glad they brought Aaron. He'll just sleep on the little pull out couch we have in the basement. I know Jack has been secretly missing all of his brothers, wondering when even one of them would be able to meet Pipsqueak. Sometimes I'm so busy needing Jack to look after me that I forget that Jack needs looking after too.

We had to wait quite awhile for their ridiculous amount of luggage to come through, and so we were a little late for the parade. That ended up being okay because I don't know if I could have lasted through the whole thing anyway, plus we were all starving and it was boiling hot. I was wearing a sundress and I could feel the sweat just rolling down my belly. Jack bought us all cold drinks, but even so, I was like a wilting flower. When it finally ended, we headed back to our house and gave them a tour. They loved Pipsqueaks room, even though Jack's dad pretended to go blind from the bright color. They brought gifts from Jack's family in Australia – and a tiny kangaroo for Pipsqueak's room. No wonder they had so much luggage, it was packed with gifts for us.

We ordered in Chinese food for supper, and visited until I thought we would all fall asleep in our chairs.

And, now here I am sitting in Pipsqueak's room having a tiny panic attack. I bought bagels and sausages and orange juice for breakfast and I'm worried that it won't be good enough. Sometimes when I'm paranoid about Jack's family, I imagine Jack and I being grandparents someday and it makes me realize that they're probably not as scary as I think they are.

I'd better get to bed though; I'm feeling sleep beginning to creep into my bones.

Ps – You should have heard the thickness of Jack's accent by the end of the night; hilarious.

Wednesday, July 2nd, 2008

There are only eight more days until my due date.

I feel like when I wake up in the morning, I can hear a booming voice counting down to something like a space shuttle launch, "EIGHT". I wonder what it would feel like to go over my due date. I hope I don't have to find out, and really, Pipsqueak could come any day now. Maybe Pipsqueak will come tomorrow, exactly one year after Tuesday's day of delivery.

I had my midwife appointment this morning and my mother in law came with me. Jack took Aaron to work, and his dad is still jet lagged and said he was hoping to grab a nap while we're gone. Sam let my mother in law listen to baby's heartbeat with the Pinard horn. Then she asked me if I'd like to be checked for progress. I told her I didn't really feel like being checked – plus it was awkward with Jack's mom there. She said there's probably not a lot of progress yet anyway, despite the fact that I have had a few hour long sessions of contractions ten minutes apart in the past couple of weeks. They never hurt though, they're just kind of exciting as my belly perks up into a hard, round little ball, and then ever so slowly, finger by finger, it unclenches and relaxes again. I made Jack feel one the other night and he was very impressed. It kind of boggles my mind when my husband looks at me like some miraculous freak of nature when my body does something strange and new and incredible.

Lately it has been so hot at night that I can barely sleep. Our room feels like a furnace. If Jack's parents weren't in the basement, Jack and I would totally move down there. I almost miss the air conditioning at the Manor, but the thought of even one more shift exhausts me, so I'll take the heat of home over air conditioned work. By three in the afternoon, I'm aching so bad that I need to go crawl in the tub to recover. My rings are getting a little tight, but I don't want to take them off. I have been trying to drink a lot of water because Sam says that staying hydrated is really important.

Tomorrow, Jack is taking his parents on a tour of the mill. I'm staying home. I have been through there before and

I'm sure it will be as hot as blazes. I'm glad I'm going to be alone too. I think that's why Jack planned their tour for tomorrow. I need some space to think.

Thursday, July 3rd, 2008

One more week; seven more days, till my due date. Seven days is how long my vigil lasted while we waited for my body to let go of Tuesday. Funny, that tiny barely formed baby still was bone of my bone... All morning I have been thinking about that horrible night when Tuesday came; and now with everyone gone, I can finally write it out.

That whole week, I felt like my ears were ringing - all outside noises were dimmed by the resounding hum reverberating in my head. I didn't know what to expect. I had never been pregnant before, I had never miscarried before.

Tuesday, the day I found out, I had thrown up that very morning before my doctor's appointment. I had not noticed any clues that there could be anything wrong with my pregnancy. The news hit me like a bucket of ice cold water, and I spent the rest of the day in a daze. I barely remember that first day. I know I didn't cook or clean – or do much of anything, other than get in my pajamas and lie sleepless in our bed.

Wednesday, I stayed in bed. Jack called in sick for both of us. He called my mom because he knew I was in no shape to be by myself, and he couldn't miss work. Mom arrived on Thursday, and I still stayed in bed. She got groceries, cleaned my house, visited with Jack in the evening – while I rotted in my stinky pajamas. On Friday, she bought me new pajamas, and washed all my sheets and bedding. I cried myself to sleep. By Sunday, we were all wondering how long this could possibly take, but that night I started getting some mild cramps and some spotting.

My house felt like a funeral home. A few friends dropped off baking. Julie phoned and talked to mom, but I refused to come to the phone. My eyes were focused inward, watching, waiting, praying, groaning and grieving.

By Monday, I could tell that my body was starting to miscarry.

Jack and I went to bed at nine, and by midnight I was writhing and moaning and crying. Jack asked what he should do – if I needed to go to the hospital, or if he should get my mom, but I didn't want anything from anyone. Maybe there was a tiny fragment of the heart of a mother that was kept alive in me that night that longed to be able to do this one thing for the child I so desperately wanted. By two in the morning, the cramps were overwhelming, and despite the care I took, there was so much blood that I had stained my new pajamas and all of our bedding. I changed, but with a sudden burst of what must have been my water breaking, I had to change again.

The blood clots were bigger than my fist, and the cramps in my stomach had me doubled over. Jack helped me find new pants three times. I started praying that I'd even see the tiny baby's body. I knew baby would only be about three centimeters long, and I wanted so badly to see – to say goodbye. At five in the morning, I passed another huge clot and suddenly, there was the baby I longed for. There wasn't a drop of blood on or around the baby. I could see hands (and later, toes and feet) – fingers, sweet little eyes; all on a person smaller than my pinky finger. I saved Tuesday's body in the small container the doctor had sent home with us from our appointment. Later, we took the tiny body to a crematorium in the city, and I watched Jack cry as he wrote the word, 'father' in the space provided for relationship to the deceased.

Once I had the baby, I thought the worst must be over. I prayed the worst was over. I felt weak, and I was covered in blood, so I climbed in the shower. Brokenly, I told Jack to go back to bed. I sat in the shower and the water wouldn't stop running red. I climbed out and got dressed again, and the cramps and waves of pain continued.

The doctor later told me it's because the baby's placenta – which Jack and I didn't think to watch for – had gotten stuck in my cervix. I started to be afraid because of the amount of blood I was seeing. I couldn't clean up the mess I had made in the shower, and I sat down on the toilet to see if my head would stop spinning. Jack got up and sat on the floor in front of me and held me as I sobbed. Slowly, the ringing in my ears got higher, and I remember not being able to see or hear. I tried to lay down on the bathroom floor as the world turned black.

Jack told me later that when he couldn't get me to respond, he ran to wake my mom. I remember waking up, and my mom leaning over me saying, "Oh, Lord, help us..." and she was wiping my face with a wet cloth. I tried to pull up my underwear – I felt ashamed and confused. Jack finally helped me get covered and I remember them talking about calling an ambulance, but Jack saying that it would be faster for him to drive me. I didn't argue about going to the hospital this time. Jack half led, half carried me to the stairs and I passed out again. I was half in and out of consciousness until he lifted me into the truck and strapped on my seatbelt. My mom was still gasping and praying in the seat between us. I didn't pass out again.

Mom had tucked a towel under me, and in minutes I had soaked through my pad, pants and through the towel too. Finally, with the hospital in sight, I passed what I thought was another clot, but later found out was the placenta; things got better (physically) from there. Jack got me a wheelchair, and took me in where they found my blood pressure was dangerously low. I was already feeling so much better though, and I wanted to go home, but they kept me for a few hours with an IV for observation and to make sure my blood pressure got back to normal.

July 3rd, 2007 – Tuesday was delivered at 5 o'clock in the morning.

de·liv·er

1. To bring or transport to the proper place or recipient.

2. To surrender (someone or something) to another; hand over.

3. To secure (something promised or desired)

4. To give birth to: She delivered a baby boy this morning.

5. To give forth or produce

6. To set free, as from misery, peril, or evil: deliver a captive from slavery.

7. To produce or achieve what is desired or expected; make good

One year ago.

There's your birth story, Tuesday.

Friday, July 4th, 2008

I had a good cry last night. Jack came home and when I didn't answer when he called for me, he left his parents in the living room and came and found me in Pipsqueak's room.

When he found me, with my puffy face, and my journal closed on my lap... I told him I was okay. He told me we're ordering in again tonight and I smiled and said, "Yum".

He stopped and turned before he walked out, and asked me one more time if I was okay – and I wasn't lying when I said that I was. I went and washed up – ate four pieces of pizza and fell asleep before my head hit the pillow.

Sunday July 6th, 2008

Pipsqueak was putting on a little show last night and Jack and I stayed up late watching. It was like a miniature fireworks display, watching little mountains rise and fall as elbows and knees poked out.

Jack cupped his mouth to my bare belly and said, "Hey, Pipsqueak, you can come out now. Your mango walls aren't that scary..."

We were tired this morning, but we went to church anyway. I was grateful for the air conditioning in the building. Every second person asked me, "How much longer?" and gave me these knowing grins, but I know nothing. I can't help but imagine that I'm counting down to the 10th, like I have been for the past nine months. I'm afraid to think of going past then.

The pastor spoke about heaven. His sermon was in broad strokes today – not the definitive nitty gritty that I often long for, and as I listened, my mind began to wander. I found myself remembering those days after we lost Tuesday. I remember people telling me, and me telling myself, that I just needed to "let go". I remember thinking that each moment, every hour, day, week, month was a vehicle propelling me light years away from the baby that I missed so badly.

Just let go – seemed like an impossible task, a ridiculous notion, a useless attempt. This morning, I finally figured out why.

I don't have to let go. I never did.

Mr. Henry's larger than life parting assignment rises up in my mind, I AM. Baby Tuesday changed the fabric of who I am. Making a futile effort to "let go" won't make anything better.

I AM changed. Tuesday is like a tiny string tying my heart to heaven. I'm not being propelled light years away from Tuesday. By God's grace, each month, week, day; every single hour, and moment... brings me closer to that place where every tear will be wiped from every eye.

I'm not forced to let go – I'm just being reminded where I'm going.

Monday, July 7th, 2008

This morning Aaron and Jack's mom and dad all helped me make my mobile for Pipsqueak. It was a complicated little project with tiny brightly colored birds on the ends of wire pieces and fake flowers. I love how it turned out. One more little item checked off my 'to do' list. Funny that I would drop my 'to do' list in a heartbeat if it meant I could meet Pipsqueak today; but the date of Pipsqueak's arrival is unknown to me, so I guess I'll just keep bumbling through, choosing chores to complete – or not – on the whim of a tiny little baby.

Jack had to go to work so my father in law and Aaron worked in the back yard, repairing and painting our tiny landing and staircase. My mother in law baked two meals for the freezer and mopped all my floors. I cleaned out every single drawer in the kitchen. Then, I folded up the maternity clothes that aren't my favorites and cleared out our closet a bit since Jack is complaining that I have four outfits in each and every imaginable size in there. It does look a lot better. After that I rewarded myself with a long soak in the tub, and watched my belly rippling in front of me. When I weighed myself today, I noticed that I lost a pound, so my total weight gain as of today is 30 pounds.

After my bath, I examined my belly extensively in the mirror. I searched for stretch marks, and finding one suspicious looking pink line, I slathered myself with more cocoa butter.

I tried to clip my toenails, but that was a miserable waste of time.

I must have phoned Jack about 50 times, but he left his cell in the truck, so didn't get any messages. I was furious with him, and when he came home, he couldn't figure out why. He said that he left me in good hands with his parents, and I wasn't even in labor! I said that wasn't the point, because what if I HAD been in labor and I couldn't get a hold of him. He promised that he'll keep his cell phone on and glued to his side from now on until Pipsqueak comes.

Tuesday, July 8th, 2008

Jack's family left today to go visit Grandma while we all wait for Pipsqueak. My mom asked if we want them to come right away, or if we want them to wait. I told her I had my midwife appointment later on today, so they should at least wait until I get a chance to talk to Sam.

I let Sam check me today, and she said I was starting to dilate just the littlest bit. I'm a "fingertip" and I guess I need to get to ten centimeters before I have the baby. She said it's impossible to tell, but that if she were a betting woman, she'd say that I still have another week to go. I could have cried.

After my appointment, Jack and I went to a Farmer's Market. We bought all kinds of fresh produce and these awesome little meat pies for supper tonight. It felt good to get out of the house and just do normal stuff. It felt good when Jack held my hand and bought me lemonade. It felt good to walk, and feel my belly harden and I'd get all out of breath. Jack flirted with me, and told me he liked my hair, and smacked me playfully from behind when I walked past.

For the afternoon, my anxiety lessened, just the tiniest bit. I felt patient, and happy, but ready.

We got home just as the clouds opened and the rain fell. Everything smells so fresh and clean after a rain fall like that.

I hope I have a baby tomorrow.

Wednesday, July 9th, 2008

I keep thinking what jobs I can do while sitting. Mostly, I vacillate between wanting to have a bath or write in my journal. Mom and Dad are coming on Saturday. They figured they'd wait till the weekend.

Every time the phone rings, or the alarm goes off, or someone knocks on the door, I feel this excitement, "Maybe something special is happening!" My mind must be foggy to leap to thoughts of childbirth from the sound of a doorbell, but there's this crushing feeling of imminence.

When I woke this morning, the space shuttle launch countdown voice boomed "ONE!!" in my head.

Will we blast off tomorrow?

Thursday, July 10th, 2008

For the first time in what feels like forever, I actually slept through the night last night. I couldn't believe it when I rubbed my puffy face this morning and realized that I'm still here, I'm still all in one piece, and I'm still very much pregnant.

Jack had to work, and I felt a sob forming in my throat as he strolled out the door. I felt almost a panicked, "What do I do now??!!" Like, after a great pilgrimage, I have arrived at my destination, and I can't find the door knob. Since this is my journal, and I feel I must be brutally honest here, I will tell you that as soon as Jack left, I walked up and down the basement stairs 20 times. I actually counted. I felt a few little tightenings, but nothing major.

Today is shaping up to be the longest day in history.

Friday, July 11th, 2008

I have taken to studying the dates on the calendar. I'm wondering which one will be significant to me in ten years time. Which of the days in the near future will be emblazoned with stars and glitter as we celebrate the birthday of our little Pipsqueak? Which day will immediately pop out of my mouth when people ask me when my baby was born? Will it be the 12th? The 13th? Please, not the 20th! What day will you choose, Pipsqueak?

Jack had to go into work again today, but he promised only to be gone for a couple of hours. Once he got home, he took me to the Manor and we picked up Essa for ice cream. I could tell she was wondering where Aaron was. It was so cute. When we went out for lunch last week with Jack's family, Aaron was so sweet with her, and I think Essa thought she hit the jackpot when she found an unmarried version of Jack. She kept holding his hand, and insisted on sitting with him at lunch. I had to remind her a couple of times to be respectful, but Aaron was such a great sport. He's such a happy kid – so unlike both Kevin and Ryan. He's the same age as they are, but so self assured and confident. He teases fearlessly, and the first night he got here, jet lag and all, he tackled Jack full on in our living room, and I thought his mom was going to have a heart attack when they finally came up for air laughing hysterically. He pushed his hair out of his eyes and grinned sheepishly, "I haven't pinned him yet, he was always so much bigger than me."

He's a lot bigger than he was the last time I saw him. He looks so much like Jack it makes me look twice when one of them walks around the corner.

I wished again that we had family closer. It's such a treat when they come to visit – feels like a little hole gets filled, and a little need is provided for.

I sure think it would be nice for Pipsqueak to have an uncle like Aaron close enough to wrestle with.

Saturday, July 12ᵗʰ, 2008

Whose baby?

Yours, Father.
i want this little gift,
This little treasure,
This little tiny baby in my arms...
But this baby belongs to You.
This one You created in the secret place –
You weaved together so intricately –

You lovingly formed from nothing.
This baby is...
Not mine.
Your design is perfect –
i know that full well.
Not my timing, my will, my plan –
Not a life borne by the will of a father and mother...
Not a mistake
But a perfect piece of what You've intended for our lives.
Yours.
Oh, Father, i ache with longing...
My heart is so tender with love...
My body is weary...
My mind is steadfast...
But, this baby remains –
Yours.

Sunday, July 13th, 2008

Mom and Dad got here on Saturday. They're just seamlessly blending into our lives. Mom knits and Dad reads his Bible. I thought I couldn't bear to go to church, but Jack convinced me that I needed to get out of the house. He said that life has to go on as we continue to wait on life.

I like that.

We snuck out before the last song and napped all afternoon.

Monday, July 14th, 2008

"I'm kind of excited for you to be 'over'." Jack grinned at me as we were getting ready for bed on Sunday night. "I'm not physically or mentally prepared yet for the baby to come..." He had a twinkle in his eye, daring me to respond, as he watched me limp into bed.

I know he's teasingly trying to keep my spirits up.

He's not the sympathetic type. The other night, we were crowded in the bath and he said, "It will be nice when we have a little more room in here again, eh?" while grabbing my wobbly hips.

I burst out laughing, "You're really gonna go there with your nine months pregnant, hormonal wife??"

He cockily answered, "I can handle you..."

Jack teases.

It's how he says, "Are you still ok? You know I love you. Only a little longer..." He has never been the compassionate, soft, emotional type of guy. He makes me stronger... much to my annoyance sometimes when I feel like being a baby - and having someone take care of me.

But - as I lean into him, my impatience melts into his patience; my irritation disappears into his humor, any pain into his strength. He's a keeper – and I'm glad he thinks it's fun to go past my due date, because apparently I have no control over the matter.

We saw Sam again today. I begged her to check me again, and I prayed for progress. She chuckled at me and assured me it doesn't work that way. She said that some women begin labor with no progress at all, while others can be 2 or 3 centimeters dilated for weeks.

I didn't care.

I wanted some kind of assurance or promise that my body was doing something. Sam grinned when she checked me. She told me that my cervix is now soft and she can stretch it to 2 centimeters.

I guess I showed her. She still booked me another appointment for Thursday. Mom said she doubts I'll make it that far. I sure hope she's right.

Tuesday, July 15th, 2008

Dad and I put up the last of the aunty and uncle baby pictures in Pipsqueaks room today. As I watched him carefully level and mount each one, I sat in my chair and talked to him. I was telling him that I think I have learned more about God in the past year than I did over the other years of my life combined. He asked what kind of things I had been learning.

I told him that when I lost Tuesday, our pastor had come to our house to see us. He had looked at my desolate face and asked me, "Are you angry with God?" I said nothing because the thought hadn't even occurred to me. He continued, "Because it's okay to be angry with Him. God is big enough to handle your hurt." Even as he spoke, and my dry mouth couldn't find the words to respond, Truth cried out from the shadows of my heart, "Anna, your Father loves you".

And He loves me still.

He loves me so much, and he is so completely trustworthy, He is so Holy, that it would be silly for me to try to stack up evidence against Him. I believed our pastor when he said, "God is big enough to handle your disappointment, anger... emotional tidal wave..." Because He is... but why rage against the One who loves me the most? Why not press into His Good Heart - and seek to follow and submit to His molding when my heart is so tender and teachable?

It reminds me of a little child who's hurt. They're angry and trying to protect their tiny wound - and as their mama reaches out to comfort them, they smack her away and flail their tender tiny bodies to the ground in despair. Yeh, mama's big enough to handle little one's anger - but her mother's heart wants to comfort - to hold and love.

I told my dad that I think God is like that. I think He wants to teach us, hold us, love us, be Our Father...if we'd just let Him. My dad grunted as he braced himself to stand and brushed the dust off his knees. He nodded at me, meeting my eyes, "I think you're right."

Wednesday, July 16th, 2008

I wish I could capture in words how much I want this little one safe in my arms. I ache for this little bun. I want to see, touch, feel, smell, hear soft cries...

Is this how my Father wants me to yearn for Him? Does He want me to ache with every fiber? Am I learning what it means to hope without seeing and to move constantly towards that reunion? ...Help me, Father.

Dear Mr. Henry –

I wanted to write you to tell you how much your class meant to me this year. Shakespeare wrote, "Give sorrow words. The grief that does not speak whispers o'er fraught heart and bids it break."

Your story met mine at a time in my life where I had no words for my sorrow. Thank you for giving me words – and for gently allowing me to learn who I am, so my heart wouldn't break.

Much love, Anna

The Story... I Am

We each have one - don't we?

The story of our lives - the sweet intermingling of different people who touched us, moved us and made us who we are; the ones who have grown alongside us - winding the vines of their story through our own, till it's impossible to tell one from the other.

i was struck the other day with the idea that -little Tuesday has a story too.

Little babe of my heart, whose brief life was lived in its entirety in my womb. My memory holds you tenderly, peaceful babe - not ready to be born. Oh, tiny one, your story is like a little vine -grafted into me.

i felt the cut when your story sliced into me - and i thought at the time- that maybe i was too damaged by that cut and that neither one of us would make it. Slowly, where you were grafted in, a little bud began to grow.

Over time, the wound no longer hurt as badly as it once did; and i felt that the graft was complete. i could hardly tell where one began and the other ended. i looked different than i would have, had you not been grafted into me. i was like a maple tree that could grow lilies, or sweet peas because of you. i could never have done that before.

Because of you, i feel like an expert gardener. The wound was gaping, but i know better now, the blessing that you have been - and i realize that you will always, always be a part of me. Not in a new age mystical way - but in the way that my Father has allowed me to be changed by a little baby that nobody else even got to meet.

Tuesday has been grafted in, and it changes forever who i am.

i am a monster tree...

My branches seem to morph before your eyes; the tendrils of my child trailing around my roots.

There is sadness - but not despair. There is longing, but it's sustained by Hope. There is a future - and it's a heavenly one. This little one causes me to keep my eyes firmly locked on my Father - who is faithful to provide what we need.

For now, i will encourage this little graft, and every leaf and branch and fiber of my being, to point to Jesus - i will allow my sorrow, and it's beautiful fruit to be seen.

A mama will never forget that which has become a part of her.

Heaven will mean finally feeling complete.

Epilogue

In the wee hours of the morning of Thursday, July 17th, Anna's water broke.

She stood, almost involuntarily still half asleep, and her low laugh woke a slumbering Jack. Tears stung her eyes as she realized that the moment she had been longing for was finally at hand. She began to chant to a still half asleep Jack, "July 17th, July 17th, Jack, it's baby day." She looked at the clock. It was 2:17 am.

He looked at her; his little bride. The heartbreak of the past year had become a permanent part of her face in the softness she now carried around her eyes. His T-shirt hung around her shoulders, and even in her roundness, she swam in it. Her yoga pants were dripping, and her face lined with sleep was radiant and ready.

He helped her find a change of clothes – such different circumstances from that terrible night a year ago – and found that he was shaking as he pulled on his own sweater to ward off the chill of the night.

Anna, wrapped loosely in fresh clothes, phoned Sam, whose warm sleepy voice calmed and soothed the chirping, hiccupping young mother on the other end of the line. As they spoke, the first tremulous contractions began to wash over Anna's body, and Sam suggested they meet at the birthing center to see what was happening.

There was a familiarity to the pain – and Anna wondered how far the similarities would go?

In a flurry of activity, Anna's parents were woken, and with an excited phone call Jack's parents too were roused from their bed as they slept miles away. Unable to return to sleep, they rose and folded their bodies together familiarly into a single chair in front of the fire until their eyes grew heavy with sleep and they fell back into semi-sleep, braving the hours of waiting ahead of them tangled in the other's arms.

As Jack grabbed her packed bag from its hiding spot, he noticed a folded piece of paper with the words, "For Jack – read in labor" scrawled in the black felt of her favorite pen. He shoved it impatiently in his jeans pocket and slung her bag over his shoulder. A tiny yellow sleeper fell out of the still unzipped bag – and he grabbed it and gruffly shoved it back inside.

Anna's mom tearfully waved from the front door as they pulled away in their truck. She stood staring after the red tail lights fading away in the night until gently her husband pulled her back in and shut the door behind him and let her sob in his arms.

When they reached the birthing center, Sam was already there with the lights burning dimly in the living room to welcome them. They walked in the door to the sounds of the tea kettle whistling, and nature sounds emitting from the stereo system. Anna asked Jack if he had brought her music and he looked at her blankly. She asked if he saw his list at the top of the bag, and he sheepishly fished it out of his pocket. The music didn't matter in the end; neither did the thick socks or the chapstick that they forgot.

After a quick check, Sam confirmed that Anna's water had indeed broken and that the contractions that were quickly becoming palpable forces were undoubtedly having an effect. She said that Anna was already three centimeters dilated.

Within an hour, each contraction rendered Anna breathless and the perspiration wet her forehead as she rocked on her hands and knees, holding onto the headboard of the king sized bed. Sam left them to get her tea, and when she peeked in on them, something about the way Anna's body sagged and groaned at the peak of her contraction prompted her to ask if Anna wanted her to run the tub.

Anna, in her concentration gave only the slightest nod, and Sam left them again in the dim room with the sounds of whale calls and ocean waves rippling through the small room in that prairie town, so far from the real ocean's roar.

Finally, leaning heavily on Jack, Anna made her way to the steaming bathroom. With her eyes still semi closed, she reached for the lights and dimmed them, then slipped out of her dress and still holding onto Jack's hand, she climbed into the water. The warm water made her feel held – supported, and comforted. She felt she could lean against it, and feel its soothing balm as she continued her labor.

It didn't take long before the minutes began to melt into one another. There was no longer any energy to be spared for the others in the room. Each contraction became its own powerful entity. Anna felt her body go into autopilot as her mind melted - unable to comprehend the earth shattering events at hand. Sam sat back on her heels, gently encouraging from the corner.

Jack's carefully worded list was lost completely, it was too dark to read it, and when he had pulled it out, he had dropped it into the water and now he found it was impossible to unfold. He had to rely on his instincts; and his love for his little wife to guide him – and they guided him well as he softly praised her efforts and sponged the sweat from her brow.

Anna was oblivious to the others in the room. She felt like she was in an alternate universe – just her and her small child. She imagined her baby descending – and she wondered, like Rita had said, if it hurt the little one to be compressed and pushed. She felt totally connected with the little one in their joint efforts to birth and to be birthed.

She felt a momentary regret as the contractions now came crashing down around her that they had forgotten the music she had prepared to listen to. As each contraction peaked and ebbed and then threatened to submerge her again, she imagined the chords and the melody and the lyrics of the music she had wanted, and shrank deeper and deeper into the water. She coped however she could; moaning and yearning for the little one coming.

Finally, time was lost completely as she felt her whole body heave and quake and break and tear... she was scared by the sheer force of it all and she wondered again how it felt for her tiny child - being birthed - as she herself was rebirthed over the course of these life altering hours on this chilly summer morn.

The contractions became unbearable - and she felt herself in urgency, begin to push. With the first push, she felt a little head descend. Rita, who had arrived only since Anna had been in the water whispered to Sam, "Do I write, 'assumed complete?'" Sam nodded and gently offered encouragement to Anna – who felt the change as her body was overcome with the primal urge to push, but still the midwives waited, patiently sitting in the corner and gently reminding Anna to "listen to her body".

How could she but listen to it as it screamed and moaned as the babe descended.

With each unbearable contraction, she bore down - and each time she was rewarded with the feeling of her baby coming nearer. Finally, Sam crept close to help guide the baby to the arms of its mother. Anna with a stunned groan felt the head crown. She hadn't known that the end was so near, and she felt the gratitude rush over her as she realized that soon, she would have her beautiful baby, her prize, in her arms.

Her body began to work independent of her mind, and each contraction fairly broke her body in two. She pushed with all her might, giving all she had to free her child. Every push wracked her frame and required far more than she was aware that she had in her to give.

Finally, a tiny body slipped from hers into the warmth of the water.

"There we go..." Sam said quietly, "Baby's comin' up your way, you got this, Anna?"

Anna reached into the water... and in that darkened room - with the sounds of chirping birds now coming from the bedroom - she pulled her daughter up from the waters and put her to her chest. Her cord pulsed between them – and Anna felt like she could hardly breathe. She couldn't even look at her - she just sank their bodies into the warmth of the water and held on. It was 9:17 am.

Finally, she managed to pull herself up – her body limp with exhaustion, to gaze at the tiny one in her arms. She looked, and beheld a lovely pink dolly. Exquisite in perfection, crying with clenched fists and impossibly dainty curled feet. Her first cries were sweet, plaintive wails and the little mother shook while she crooned at her daughter in those first precious moments that were the beginning.

"Summer, may the Lord bless you and keep you;"

Jack began to pray the prayer of blessing they had planned for their tiny child – including the name they had chosen weeks before, should they be given a daughter.

"May the Lord show you his kindness,

and have mercy on you.

May the Lord watch over you,

and give you peace."

For more of Paige's writings visit her blog:

http://sojourner-ephraim.blogspot.com

Cover art

I was inspired to paint this simple picture, by all the bereaved women who participate in the annual Walk to Remember at the Alberta Legislature. I was struck with the fact that legislation alone will never effect the change in public opinion about the value of children. The gentle act of a bereaved mother releasing a balloon...with a name attached... accompanied by a prayer...kindly spoken or written words... shared tears...these are poignant and powerful tools.

For more information go to:

http://www.walktoremember.ca

Shirley Sloan

7748401R0

Made in the USA
Charleston, SC
06 April 2011